FETCHING

___

KYLIE GILMORE

Cover design by: Michele Catalano Creative

Cover photographer: Wander Aguilar

Cover Model: Forest Harrison

Dog: Chuy

Published by: Extra Fancy Books

ISBN-13: 978-1-64658-021-7

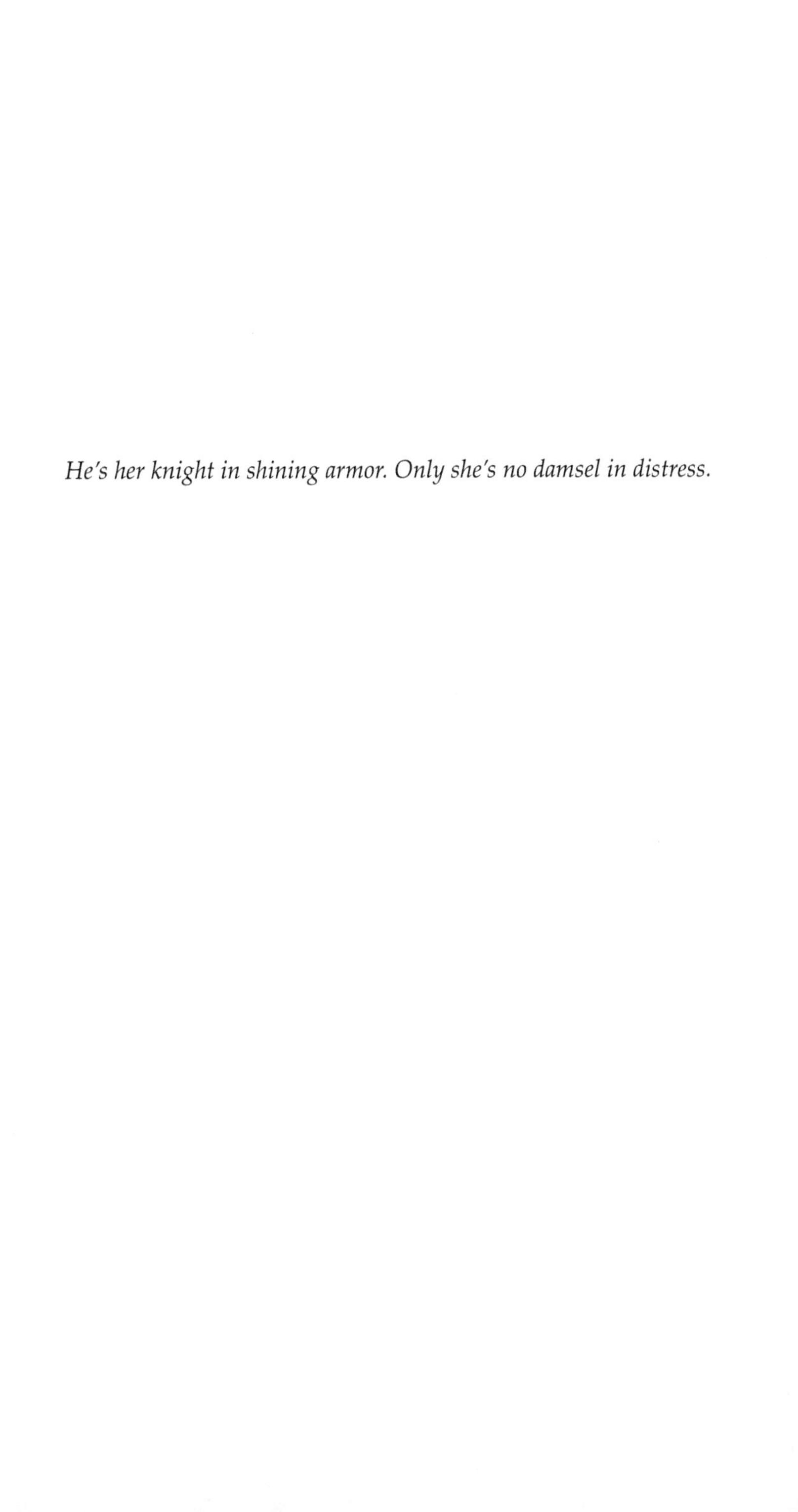

He's her knight in shining armor. Only she's no damsel in distress.

1

———

Sydney

Satan walks into my bar and crooks his finger at me.

I pretend not to see. Wyatt Winters can flag down someone else to serve him. I don't care if tonight is make-or-break time for the historic restaurant and bar I own, and this New Year's Eve fundraiser party is my last hope. I will *not* consort with the devil.

He's handsome, all right, with his thick wavy dark brown hair, sensual lips, trimmed beard, and a body that looks like he spends too much time at the gym. But that is all cancelled out by his smug attitude. Wyatt moved to town a month ago, buying the abandoned house on the top of the hill with a landlocked lighthouse. It was originally owned by an eccentric recluse, who died before I was born. People say it's haunted. I hope the ghosts keep him up at night.

Seriously, why does Wyatt keep showing up at my beloved Horseman Inn? Over the last month, he's ordered every beer I have on tap and criticized the quality at length, as well as complained about the chill in the room and, of all things, the name of the place. It's historic! The inn dates back to 1788 when it used to be a stagecoach stop.

I slip behind the bar and fill another round of drink orders for the table of middle-aged women excitedly anticipating our guest of honor, my famous actress friend, Harper Ellis. She's the only reason we have a crowd tonight. My younger brother provides chill background music on his acoustic guitar. The bar is packed, the back room is half full, and people are helping themselves to appetizers in the front dining room and bidding on the silent auction items. It's early yet, so I'm thrilled with the crowd. *Thank you, Harper.*

Harper and I grew up together here in Summerdale, New York, a lakeside community about an hour and a half outside New York City. It's a unique place, originally founded by hippies as a kind of utopia. Crime is low and quality of life is high—our unofficial motto. Actual motto: Peace for all sheltered within. Anyway, it's an awesome community for those of us not about to go bankrupt. Harper offered to help me out, but I'm not going there for several reasons. Most importantly, I don't want money to come between us.

I hope she gets here soon. I scan the back room quickly and catch the eye of the one man who sets me on edge like no other. *No beer for you.* I take the tray of wine and two dirty martinis to the women sitting at a long rectangular table across from the man I refuse to acknowledge. I serve the women their drinks, keeping my back to Satan.

"When does Harper get here?" Tammy, a brunette in her fifties, asks.

Her four friends look to me eagerly.

"Any minute, I'm sure. She's probably caught in city traffic."

"I'm the current high bid on the lunch with her," Tammy says. "Fingers crossed!"

I smile. It was nice of Harper to throw that lunch in there, considering she's such a private, shy person in real life.

Tammy's friends chime in with their hopes for winning an autographed picture of Harper or some of the other items she donated from her old TV show. She was so generous with her contributions, but I need her here in person.

"I'll let you know as soon as she arrives," I say.

I wave to my two best friends, Jenna and Audrey, mingling in the front room. They're opposites physically—

Jenna is tall and lean with blond hair that barely touches her shoulders; Audrey is short and curvy with long black hair. The four of us—me, Harper, Jenna, and Audrey—used to spend all our time together as kids. Then Harper left for Hollywood, and life happened for the rest of us. Jenna and I recently moved back to town. Audrey never left.

I send them a questioning look. They're looking out for Harper.

Jenna shakes her head. I suppress a sigh and turn to head back to the bar.

"Cindy, over here," a deep baritone voice calls out.

I stiffen and slowly turn to Wyatt. "It's Sydney," I say through my teeth.

He cups a hand by his ear. "What?"

I exhale sharply and cross to his corner table tucked in the back. He's around my age (I'm twenty-eight), wearing a black and white checked button-down shirt with a tan sport coat and jeans. His long legs are stretched out under the table, crossed at the ankles. Dark brown leather shoes instead of sneakers. It occurs to me he dressed nice for the party, only to sit alone on New Year's Eve. I summon patience and all the goodwill I can muster. He's new in town, and I should try to make him feel welcome.

"Hi, Wyatt." I flash a quick smile. "It's *Sydney*, not Cindy." *As I've told you before.* "I know you're new in town. I could introduce you to my brothers. That's Eli on guitar. He's a cop." I point him out, and Eli jerks his chin at us. "Over at the bar, the guy in the white T-shirt with the scowl is my oldest brother, Drew. There's also Adam and Caleb, but they're not here yet."

Wyatt cocks his head. "No sisters?"

"No, why?"

"Only girl, huh? Interesting."

I hear an insult lurking in his tone. "Why is that interesting?" I'm not a girly girl, but that doesn't mean I'm not feminine. I'm wearing lipstick, and I even put on a skirt tonight. It's black leather to match my knee-high black leather boots. My black T-shirt says The Horseman Inn, our staff uniform.

"Just interesting," he says blithely. "I've met Adam. He's going to do some work at my place."

"Oh." Adam is a master carpenter. I didn't know he took a job for Satan.

He taps the dark wood table. "What I really want to know is what a guy has to do to get a decent beer around here."

Patience. Goodwill. I can't be alienating customers in my line of work. I paste on a smile and rattle off every beer we offer, both on tap and in bottles.

He rubs his dark beard. "Do you have one that doesn't taste like it's been watered down to disguise the fact it's gone skunk?"

"All of our beers are fresh, I assure you. Now what can I get you?" I am Miss Hospitality.

He leans forward, resting his chin on his hand, and smiles wolfishly. My pulse shoots up. "Surprise me."

Cheap lite beer with a shot of spit in it, coming right up! Ooh, I am so tempted. No, I can be professional. *Why is my pulse still racing?* "You got it. Our best IPA coming up." I turn to go.

"I've had your best IPA," he says. "An ale would be an improvement. I hope."

I turn back. "No problem."

"Also, my table is wobbly." He gives it a shake.

I let out a breath. "Then don't shake it."

He peers under the table. "Actually, I'm not sure if it's the table or the wavy hardwood floor."

"Part of our charm, original eighteenth-century flooring."

He arches a brow.

"One ale coming up." I make a beeline to the bar, my patience running out. No one could keep up pleasant conversation with a man like that for long. Always looking for flaws. This place has all the historic charm with all the modern headaches—sloping floors, low ceilings, draftiness. I'm proud to say we still have the original post and beam ceilings and large stone hearth in the front dining room. If he doesn't like it, he can go someplace else. Although we are the only bar around for miles. He'd have to cross the state line into Clover Park, Connecticut, about a half-hour drive from here, to find another bar. Maybe I'll suggest it. No, I can't do that. He's a newcomer. *Must be welcoming.*

My brother Drew grabs my upper arm as I swing by him at the bar, halting me. "That guy bothering you?" he asks in a low voice, his gaze narrowing on Wyatt. Drew is five years older than me and a certified badass—former Army Ranger with a black belt. He runs his own dojo in town. He'll kick ass on my behalf, but I'm no damsel in distress. Besides, I grew up with brothers—two older, two younger—I know how to handle men.

"He's just annoying," I say. "No problem."

He releases my arm. "Say the word."

I give him an exaggerated smacking kiss on his cheek, which always throws him.

He rubs the spot. "Syd! Come on. Is there pink on my cheek?"

I sail behind the bar. "So much pink," I lie. "Better head to the men's room to get properly manly again." It's actually coral, a darker shade of pink to go with my auburn hair, but try explaining lipstick shade to a grumpy alpha male.

He checks himself with his phone's camera and huffs, tucking the phone back in his jeans' pocket. "Smart-ass."

I pour Wyatt's ale and then check on a few customers at the bar, filling their drinks too. Mostly as a stalling tactic so I don't have to deal with Mr. Big City Snark yet. I heard Wyatt moved here from Manhattan. Why? Why couldn't he have stayed in the city?

I flag down one of our servers and pass Wyatt's drink to her. It's self-preservation. The less I interact with him, the better the chance I don't dump a drink on his head. That wouldn't be very hospitable of me.

After I check on things in the kitchen for the upcoming buffet dinner, I take another tour through the restaurant, making sure everyone's enjoying drinks and appetizers, and reminding them of the fab silent auction items. I work hard to sound upbeat about the auction instead of desperate. My father left this place in such debt before his passing, no bank will give me a loan. Nasty surprise, that debt. He hid his financial troubles from me and my brothers out of some misguided need to protect us. He was a great dad, though, and stepped up after my mom passed when I was twelve.

Wyatt catches my eye. "Appetizers are good."

Pleased that he *finally* said something positive about my place, I close the distance, stopping at his table. "Glad you're enjoying them."

He leans back in his chair. "Have you ever thought of upgrading the dinner menu?"

My temper flares, but I manage to keep a civil tone. "No. Locals love it."

"Not saying it's bad, just unoriginal. I mean, every meal comes with either French fries or baked potato. A new chef might bring some life to the place. Isn't that what tonight's fundraiser's all about? Keeping this place open?" He taps the table. "With the right management, a better chef, this place has potential."

I manage this place, and the chef is a family friend. I bare my teeth. "Seems you know a lot about the restaurant business."

"Not at all. I just appreciate a good one."

I jam my hands on my hips and glare at him. *Obviously he thinks we're a bad one!* I'm so furious I can't even speak.

He cocks his head. "Cindy, are you cross with me?"

"Who the hell do you think you are?" I snap. "Coming in here and insulting my place left and right! If you don't like it, don't come back."

He arches a brow. "Since you own the place, maybe we could talk about some serious improvements. You don't know what you don't know, am I right?"

I bristle. "This place was my great-grandfather's, passed down the generations, and now it's mine." I leave out that Drew is the one who actually inherited it and declared it a lost cause because of the debt dragging it down. I took it over rather than let him sell it. "It's an institution in this town, and we're doing just fine without your city snark. How dare you walk in here and spew your judgment over all of us!"

He smirks. "I don't recall spewing."

My heartbeat roars in my ears, anger clouding all good reason. I desperately want to smack that smirk off his face.

He gestures to his ale, which he barely touched. "I didn't like this one. Could I get one of those local Connecticut ales you mentioned?"

I stare at his glass of ale. I want to throw it in his face and watch his shock as it drips down his beard, fancy sport coat, and dress shirt.

He chuckles. "That's an evil look in your eye, Cindy. You're thinking about dumping this drink on my head, aren't you?"

How did he know? "Not at all," I lie.

He leans close and smirks. "I dare you."

Oh no he didn't. He's deliberately baiting me. I work for a cool collected tone. "It's too bad you didn't like your ale because that is the last drink you're ever getting here."

"Just because I said with a better chef this place has potential?"

It was that and a pile of other insults. I'm so done with this guy. I don't care if he's a newcomer and alone on New Year's Eve. I turn on my heel and nearly run into Harper and her fiancé, Garrett, who probably heard everything.

"Syd, are you okay?" Harper asks, her brows furrowing over concerned hazel eyes. She's wearing her dark brown curls down and her skin glows with good health.

I give her a hug. "So happy to see you!" I pull back. "You too, Garrett. I've got a table reserved just for you." I gesture for them to follow me and head over to it, relieved to get away from that arrogant, critical, evil man. I will forever after refer to him as Wart. Satan is too good for him.

I take the small reserved sign off the table and realize they haven't followed me. They're sitting with Wyatt, talking to him. Harper holds up a finger for me to wait. Does he know them, or did he just invite them to join him? Harper *is* a very popular actress. Everyone wants to talk to her.

Wart winks at me, saying in a loud voice, "Right, *Sydney*." I don't catch the rest of what he says. I bet Harper corrected him calling me Cindy. *Grr...*

I bend over and slap my ass at him. *Screw you, Wart!*

Harper gasps and hurries over to me. "What are you doing? Don't you know who that is?"

"Yeah, Wyatt." *The smug asshole who insulted my father's legacy.*

She leans close and whispers, "Didn't you get my email?"

I stare at her, confused. We emailed quite a bit about tonight's fundraiser. "Which one?"

She puts a hand on my arm, her voice taking on an urgent tone that has the hair on the back of my neck rising. "About who he is and what he can do for you."

"No, I didn't get any email about him." My voice is barely above a whisper. I clear my throat. "It must've went to junk or got lost in cyberspace. Who is he?"

"He's a retired billionaire with experience turning around failing businesses. I met him at a fundraiser and told him about Summerdale. He wanted somewhere to lie low and chill. Anyway, I might've mentioned that The Horseman Inn needs help." At my stunned silence, she goes on in a rush. "Don't be mad, okay? You refused to accept a loan from me, which I get because we're friends, but I couldn't just do nothing. He could help you." She shakes her head. "I can't believe you slapped your ass at him."

I stare at her. "But he's so young to be a retired billionaire."

"I know. He's one of those tech whiz guys. Made his first million at nineteen. He's thirty now."

I slowly turn to meet the knowing, smirky eyes of retired billionaire Wyatt "the Wart" Winters. He grins and gives me a jaunty two-finger salute, probably because he knows Harper just explained who he is. Mr. Big Shot.

I scowl. I will *never* work with that man. I don't care how many zeroes are in his bank account or what kind of business guru he is. He wants a piece of The Horseman Inn? Hell no!

2

I retreat behind the bar and get started on a margarita. I don't need Wyatt Winters. I have a marketing background. Once I get out of debt, then I'll be able to focus on marketing to draw people from neighboring towns, and that will revitalize the place. I know it can still be a success. Though, if tonight's fundraiser isn't a success, I sure as hell need some kind of bailout.

I keep myself busy filling drink orders, but my mind keeps cranking over every insult Wart delivered in the past month and what I wish I could've said. Being in the restaurant business, you just can't lay into rude customers, no matter how much they deserve it. All things considered, I held my temper admirably until tonight.

"Hey, Sydney."

I look up at Garrett's warm voice. Harper's fiancé is a beast of a man with plenty of muscle and a heart of gold. Seriously, he drove all the way from Brooklyn a few days ago to fix some stuff in the restaurant's kitchen for me and refused to take payment.

"Hey, Garrett," I say, giving him an affectionate punch on the shoulder. "What can I get you?"

He grabs one of the menus, scans it, and then orders an ale. That's the ale Wart wanted earlier. I'm instantly suspicious he's going to take it to Wart, but I don't want to say anything in case it's actually for Garrett. He fixed a leaking dishwasher and an exhaust fan that was on its last legs, making a weird grinding noise. Garrett can do just about anything in construction, that's his main job, and he's getting some acting gigs on the side now. Now why couldn't I meet someone fun, interesting, and competent like that? Why does Wart have to be the only single option around? He's so irritatingly gorgeous too with those warm light brown eyes—whiskey eyes—and the beard. That big muscular body. My pulse got crazy when we got close.

This is terrible. I'm involuntarily drawn to him. I should see a shrink or something.

I hand over the glass of ale to Garrett, restraining myself from ordering him not to give it to Wart. "Here you go."

He flashes a smile. "Thanks." He reaches for his wallet.

"On the house for your help fixing stuff for me."

He shakes his head. "I like fixing stuff." He leaves a twenty on the bar and walks away.

"Thanks again," I call. "I owe you."

He waves over his shoulder, like it's nothing. What a great guy.

I tell myself not to look, but I can't help it. My eyes are glued to Garrett as he makes his way back to Wart's table. Dammit! I knew it! He slides the ale over to Wart, who immediately lifts it in a gloating toast to me.

I clench my teeth, my entire face heating with anger.

Wyatt takes a sip of ale and makes an exaggerated grimace. "Do the locals like this watered-down stuff?" His voice carries all the way to me, as I'm sure was his intention.

I throw up my middle finger, and then it doesn't feel like enough, so I add the other in a double *fuck you* salute.

He throws his head back and laughs.

I silently seethe until I'm elbowed by my bartender, Betsy. Apparently, I'm in her way, having a quiet fit behind the bar.

I go back to work, frequently checking on the action around Harper and steadfastly avoiding eye contact with Wart. She's sitting at her reserved table, signing autographs on New Year's Eve flyers from tonight's event, and taking selfies with customers.

After a large crowd leaves her table, I dash over to check in with her. "What can I get you to drink, Harp? Anything you want, on the house."

She smiles. "Water would be great."

"Just water?"

She gives my shoulder a tug, pulling me closer to whisper, "I'm pregnant."

I squeal and hug her. "I'm so happy for you! Congratulations!"

Jenna and Audrey join us, both of them wearing glittery tiaras and cute black dresses. "What's all this squealing about?" Jenna asks.

"I told you not to fangirl over Harper," Audrey says to me. "She's still one of us."

Harper whispers the news to them.

"That is squeal-worthy," Jenna says with a laugh, hugging Harper.

Audrey hugs her next. "Congratulations!" She pulls back, looking concerned. "How did your grandmother take it?"

Harper was raised by her tough grandmother, who might not approve of a pregnancy before the wedding. We secretly call her General Joan. Once in a while, the General comes in here for an early dinner, and I always find myself stiff with shoulders back, spine straight. She never had a problem ordering Harper's friends around, same as Harp. I guess that means she loves us too.

Harper beams. "Surprisingly understanding and supportive. We had a good talk." She hitches a thumb at Garrett, who just joined us. "It helps that the General *loves* him."

"What's your secret?" Jenna asks Garrett. "We were all scared of her as girls. Half the time she put us to work."

Audrey shakes her head. "We never wanted to hang at Harper's house. No offense, Harp."

"That was probably her plan all along," Harper says. "Not to have to clean up after four girls."

"She put me to work too," Garrett says with a smile. "I don't mind helping out."

We all stare at him.

"Now I feel so lazy," I quip.

Everyone laughs.

"It's really hopping now, Syd," Harper says.

I nod. "They're here for you." There's about fifty people here now. Normally, there's a dozen or less.

A couple in their thirties approaches, asking for her autograph. Harper smiles. "Happy to."

Jenna pulls me toward the bar. "Let's get some of those peppermintinis." It's a special peppermint martini just for the holidays.

I head back toward the bar with Jenna and Audrey, passing my oldest brother, Drew, on the way. He's acting strange, just standing there, a beer in hand, not responding in any way to my brother Caleb, who's speaking animatedly to him. Drew's eyes lock on Audrey.

I watch Audrey as I head behind the bar. She's carefully avoiding looking at Drew. Even stranger. Normally, she'd say hello and smile. Audrey has had a thing for Drew since we were kids. She emailed him regularly through his military deployments, but never told him how she felt. Did something happen between them recently? Audrey isn't the kind to broadcast every little thing, even to her friends, especially if it's a sensitive topic.

Audrey walks stiffly past Drew, head held high. He just stares, his expression shuttered.

She and Jenna take a seat at the bar, a short distance from Drew. I'm sure if there were any other seats available, Audrey would've dashed for them.

I lean over the bar toward Audrey. "Peppermintini?"

"Sure," she says distractedly, staring off in the distance. I always think Audrey has a lot more in her head than what comes out of her mouth.

I get started on my friends' peppermintinis, glancing over at Drew. He stares at his beer, lifts his head, and gives Caleb a clap on the shoulder.

"Looks like everyone's keeping Harper busy," Jenna says, reaching up to check her glittery tiara and smoothing her blond hair down.

I give the martini shaker a shake. "Oh, yeah. Everyone mostly wants to hear about her old show *Capital Asset*."

"Well, it's what made her famous." She turns to Audrey, who's still staring off in the distance. "You okay?"

"Of course," Audrey says brightly.

Jenna and I exchange a look. Audrey moved to town in first grade, and we're as close as sisters, which means we know she's lying. Something is bothering her, and it has to do with Drew. Did she finally tell him how she feels? If she did, it must not have gone the way she hoped.

I meet Audrey's blue eyes with a sympathetic look. Jenna gives Audrey's arm a squeeze.

Audrey twirls a lock of her long black hair, feigning nonchalance. "Stop staring at me. I'm fine. Everything's okay. Nothing's new."

I pour out a martini. Awfully defensive for someone who claims to be just fine. I'll get it out of her at our next Thursday night book club meeting, which I've officially dubbed the Thursday Night Wine Club because who are we kidding?

I slide over the two drinks, refusing payment because they helped me plan this whole night, but Jenna slides a twenty-dollar bill onto the bar anyway, giving me a little air kiss. Audrey follows suit.

A short while later, the buffet is ready in the front room for the main dinner courses. I make sure Harper, Garrett, and her bodyguard, Joe, get their meal delivered to their table before directing the crowd to line up for their meal. Everything's going as smoothly as I could hope. I go back in the kitchen to check on things and finally give myself a break, taking a seat on a stool in the corner and eating my own dinner of chicken wings, French fries, and carrot sticks.

By the time it's near midnight, I'm dead tired. Between all of my duties and trying to rein in my temper, it's been an exhausting night. One last burst of energy to keep up the festive spirit. *One, two, three, go!*

I hand out Happy New Year sunglasses and party horns to the people sitting at the bar and weave through the crowd in the back room, giving out favors with a smile. When I get to Wart's table, I give Garrett the favors and skip Wart completely. He clutches his chest like he's wounded. Garrett looks between us two with a small smile on his face. *Has Wart been trash-talking me?* He deserves everything I dished out tonight. And I restrained myself too. I didn't dump a beer on his head, now did I?

I make it back to my friends' table, where Harper is now sitting. "Happy New Year's, ladies! May it be our best yet." I hand out the favors.

Jenna and Audrey put on the New Year's glasses and blow their horns at me.

Harper surprises me by standing to whisper in my ear, "Syd, I know Wyatt rubbed you the wrong way, but he's actually a good guy."

I snort. "Right."

"Anyway, happy New Year." She kisses my cheek.

I continue my relentlessly upbeat tour of tables, handing out party favors.

Five minutes before midnight, I flop down in the seat next to Harper and hand her a glass of sparkling water, the pregnant woman's champagne. "I'm going to count down for the New Year's toast, unless you'd like to do it."

"Nah, you're the star of this show."

I put my arm around her, and she rests her head on mine. "Thanks for coming, Harp. The auction is doing great. Someone bid a thousand dollars to have lunch with you."

"Really? Last I saw, it was at a hundred fifty."

I pull away and grin. "Well, you are Harper Ellis."

"Stop," she says.

I sock her on the shoulder and head over to Eli on guitar to let him know he's off duty. As soon as he leaves his post, I stand on his chair and wave for attention.

Garrett stands and lets out a sharp whistle, and the crowd settles down. He strides over to Harper's table, and all eyes follow him as he crosses the room. He takes a seat and drops an arm around her shoulders. They're quite a beautiful couple.

I gesture toward them. "Let's all give a big round of applause for our hometown star Harper Ellis!"

Polite applause rings out. Harper smiles and waves at everyone. I feel like they could've shown more enthusiasm, but don't want to beg for applause on her behalf.

I continue. "I know you all love The Horseman Inn as much as I do, so I hope you'll stop by in the new year to check out our new appetizer menu." *Take that, Wart!* I was so angry I forgot to use that as a comeback when he criticized our dinner menu. We added five new appetizers. "We'll be sponsoring a fun trivia night every Friday, starting this Friday, and, ladies, half-price drinks on Thursday nights starting next week!" We're closed tomorrow for New Year's Day. It's pretty dead in town that day, and I wanted to give the staff the day off.

The women applaud and cheer enthusiastically.

"What about the guys?" Wyatt asks. "Which night is half-price drinks for us?" He lifts both palms as if to say *you forgot about us poor billionaire guys.*

I narrow my eyes.

"Ten seconds!" Harper calls out, saving me from telling Wart off in front of everyone.

"Right," I say brightly, checking my phone. "Here we go!" I count down at the top of my lungs. "Five, four, three, two, one! Happy New Year!" I blow my horn, and then the room erupts in horn blowing.

Except Wart, whom I didn't give a horn. He does a slow clap, smiling at me, looking positively devilish. He cups his hands around his mouth and shouts over the noise of the crowd, "Happy New Year, Cindy!"

"Happy New Year, Wart!"

I join my friends, ignoring his bark of laughter.

3

Wyatt

I've been nosing around Sydney Robinson's business, the oddly named Horseman Inn, at my friend Harper's urging and came to the conclusion that, while Sydney is incredibly entertaining, she'd be impossible to work with. I could help her out, but let's face it, her type—hot-tempered and fiery—is great in bed not in business. And I wouldn't mind if my bed is exactly where she lands.

In the meantime, I can't seem to help pushing her buttons. She cracks me up. Most people kiss my ass because they want my money. She gestured for me to kiss hers. I look forward to seeing what she'll come up with next. I am one sick puppy.

Speaking of…

Snowball races to the front window, her paws scrabbling on the sheets covering the original hardwood floors in the fixer-upper I bought. She's a seven-year-old shih tzu with a mostly white coat and a few tan and dark gray markings. Not a puppy, but with her small size and big black eyes, she still has that puppy appeal. She's attached to me, so I had to adopt her.

I walk over in my bare feet, following her to the front window, and spot Bill, the mailman, making a trip out here just for me. It's New Year's Day, which means the post office is closed. And it's snowing another layer on top of what we had. I appreciate him coming out here today. Snowball barks urgently—someone has crossed the perimeter of our domain.

"Stand down, Snowball."

Bill's tamales were a major selling point for me when Harper first told me about this quirky lakeside community. A mailman who delivers tamales along with the mail. Does it get any better than that? Imagine my disappointment when we first met a month ago and he told me the tamales were only a spring and fall happening. Winter made the tamales cold on arrival, and summer heat destroyed them. We worked out a monthly deal for the off-season. He's fantastic at what he does. I keep telling him he should open a food truck by the lake.

Snowball quiets, her white eyebrows lifting over big dark eyes as she gives me her *desperate for food* look. Or it could be extreme concern that I told her to stand down when there's clearly someone on the property. I don't know. I don't speak shih tzu. I go with the most important point.

"No, you can't have any. Tamales are not dog food."

I head over to the front door, and she trots by my side. My mouth is already watering. This is my second delivery of tamales, and I've been thinking about eating them for lunch ever since I woke up.

I scoop Snowball under one arm just before I open the door in advance of Bill's knock. She's not used to all the open space here after our Manhattan apartment, and I don't want her to get lost out there in the snow. I smile at my tamale-delivering pal. "There's the man of the hour."

Bill's cheeks are ruddy from the cold. He's a middle-aged white guy wearing a gray cap with earflaps and a navy wool coat. When I first heard about the tamales, I'd hoped for a Mexican community here. I love Mexican food, the spicier the better. Nope. Just Bill here cooking up tamales. I'll be eating these all week and happy to do so.

"Happy New Year, Wyatt. Hello, Snowball." He hands me

a foil-wrapped package of twenty tamales. "Still warm, I hope."

"Thanks. Feels like it." Snowball's nose works double time as she leans toward the package to sniff.

Bill gives her a scratch behind the ears. "Aren't you a pretty girl?"

Snowball leans into his touch, which speaks volumes. She doesn't like just anyone, and she'll growl to let them know where they stand in her opinion. She's a good people barometer.

I hold up the tamales. "I've been looking forward to these all day. You want to join me for lunch?"

He smiles, shaking his head. "My wife's got an early New Year's Day dinner planned. She won't be happy if I fill up on tamales. I'd better go. Enjoy."

"I'm telling you, Bill, a food truck down by the lake, featuring these tamales, would kill it. People would drive from miles around to get these."

He waves that away. "I know *you* would. See you."

"One day, I'm telling you."

He leaves, whistling a happy tune.

I shut the door, set Snowball down, and head to my newly remodeled kitchen. White cabinets with simple silver bar pulls, light gray granite countertops, and a center island, also topped with light gray granite, with cabinet space underneath. The heated floor is large white and gray square tiles. First thing I did when I bought the place was have it cleaned top to bottom, pulled out old carpet, and replaced all the wallpaper with a neutral cream paint. Then I moved in while the contractors renovated the kitchen and bathroom. Now my 1920s house reminds me of a cozy bed-and-breakfast. I have plans for a library, a larger living room, and a master bedroom suite. Once the permits come through, I'm also adding two more bathrooms.

This place used to be a farm. The property has acres of woodland, rolling grassy hills, a large chunk of flat land, and a pond. It hasn't been farmed in a long time. I'm having a blast with it. It's the first time I've owned a fixer-upper, and I get to dig into historic architecture to do it. The best part is the landlocked lighthouse on the property. You can see it from all over town since I'm at the top of a hill. I'm not even close to Lake Summerdale, which is only big enough for canoes and rowboats anyway. No big ships approaching. Ha-ha. I appreciated the irony of a lighthouse on dry land, so I bought the house.

A few minutes later, I set a plate of three tamales down at my rectangular wood kitchen table, with a glass of milk, napkin, fork, and knife. Snowball settles next to my chair to watch, lying down, as she knows is polite. I never feed her at the table, but she's always hopeful I might accidentally drop some food. I carefully peel back the corn husk surrounding the tamale and slice off a piece. I pop it into my mouth, closing my eyes and groaning over how good it is. The sauce bursts with spicy heat combined with melted cheese, shredded pork, and a delicious corn masa. Perfection.

I moved to Summerdale on Harper's recommendation, who grew up here. She described it as a dinky town no one's ever heard of. Sounded like a great place to lie low and chill. I wanted that because I'm tired of fake friends with their hand out and the constant fundraiser circuits. I contribute behind the scenes now, mostly anonymously in the form of donations, but I've also helped turn around some failing businesses. Only if I'm comfortable with my business partner. They can't be a money-grubber who's going to spend it on themselves and let the business go down the drain. That's why I insist on some control. I'm one of those people who can see the forest for the trees instantly. And I get the job done.

Besides the occasional business project and playing renovation supervisor here, I'm officially retired after several lucrative tech startups. Most recently I sold my virtual reality system to a certain social media company who was willing to pay handsomely for it. And I created and sold a few other tech companies before that.

I take a drink of milk and meet Snowball's soulful eyes. She worships me. "Good girl," I murmur before taking another bite of tamale.

I lived in California for a while, hanging with the other Silicon Valley whiz kids, got invited to fancy parties, including a few in Hollywood. Briefly dated an actress—nightmare. The woman would barely eat and was all drama all the time. Eventually, I moved to Manhattan to be closer to family. I'm the man of the family ever since my dad died when I was thirteen. My three younger sisters are in their twenties now, but that doesn't mean they don't need me. Two of them live in New Jersey, where we grew up, and one in Manhattan.

Snowball races out of the room, barking. Strange. I don't know many people in town yet, and she's not a big barker. Maybe Bill came back for something. I stand, taking one last longing look at my lunch before leaving it. No one else knows about my hidden lair out here in the suburbs of New York except my family. *Crap.* An in-person visit with no notice means one of my sisters was too upset to do anything but act on instinct. They know I'll take care of whatever it is. It's not a problem with our mom, or I would've gotten multiple texts and phone calls from all three sisters. Besides, Mom's in her prime, climbing mountains and hiking in her fifties.

I reach the front window, order Snowball to stand down, and watch as my youngest sister's red Jeep comes to a halt behind my silver BMW SUV. Kayla sits there, inspecting herself in the rearview mirror and then applying makeup under her eyes.

My hands form fists. She was crying, probably for a long time if she's trying to cover up bags under her eyes. Who upset her? I bet it was some loser who doesn't deserve her. I'll kick his ass.

She steps out of the Jeep, wearing a red down jacket over jeans and black boots. Her dark brown hair flies around her face in the wind. She pushes her hair back in place as she approaches the front door, muttering to herself.

I wait for her to ring the bell. She has a habit of talking to herself when she's working through something.

I wait and wait, but she doesn't ring it. I scoop up Snowball and open the front door just as Kayla's turned to go back to her Jeep.

"Kayla! Where are you going?"

She freezes, her back to me, but I can tell she's wiping tears off her cheeks. I'm very familiar with sisterly tears. Also, high-pitched squeals and laughter bordering on the insane. That is, when the three of them are together. It's a wonder I still have my hearing.

I blow out a breath of exasperation because she still hasn't moved, her back to me. "I know you're crying, so you don't have to put on a happy face. Get in here, runt." Youngest, smallest, of course I call her runt.

She turns, her face crumbling. "Oh, Wyatt."

I move swiftly, my bare feet stinging with the cold of the snow, wrapping my arm around her shoulders and guiding her inside. "Don't worry. I've got tamales."

She laughs through her tears, and we head inside together.

Never let it be said that tamales can't fix everything. Bad investment? Tamales. Squashed your pinky toe? Tamales. Broken heart? Tamales. I've dealt with the first two before in the tamale way, and I suspect Kayla is dealing with that last one. As far as I know, everything is going well with her graduate studies, and she's living at home to save money, so it's not any kind of professional or financial issue.

She sets her fork down after her second tamale, finishes her milk, and gives me a small smile. "I didn't realize how hungry I was until I smelled these delicious tamales. Did you make them?"

"Ha. No. You know I'm not a big cook."

She lifts one shoulder. "I figured maybe you had time on your hands now that you're retired."

"It was the mailman."

She blinks her big brown eyes. "Really?"

"Yeah. So what's up?"

She gathers our dishes, avoiding my eyes. "Nothing much."

"Uh-huh."

She takes them to the sink, runs water over them, and sets them in the dishwasher.

I tip my wooden chair back, balancing on two legs. "Would you like to tell me why you've been crying for days?"

She bows her head for a moment before turning to face me. "It hasn't been days."

"Tell that to your face."

She shakes her head, walks over, and gives my face a shove. My chair nearly topples back. I right the chair, grabbing her arm for balance.

"You nearly put me out of commission!" I bark.

She sits next to me again. "Mom always told you not to lean back in your chair or you'll fall backwards."

"My house. My chair. My choice to risk my ass on the floor. Besides, you shoved me."

She sighs.

That's a precursor to a flood of words, so I let it ride, telling myself to savor the calm before the storm.

She stares at the table, using her index finger to push a small tamale crumb around. Snowball perks up, hoping for a scrap, and comes out from under the table to sit by Kayla.

"Hello, Snowball," she coos, scooping her up and snuggling into her soft fur. Snowball lifts her head, sniffing Kayla's face for tamale, and licks her cheek. She holds her close and finally drops the bomb. "I was supposed to get married last night. It was going to be so romantic on New Year's Eve, start the New Year with a beautiful bang, and then he never showed up." Her voice chokes at the end.

I right my chair, anger and hurt warring inside me. I keep my voice calm. "Why didn't you tell me you were getting married?" I'm supposed to be the one walking her down the aisle. She's six years younger, which means she's always looked up to me. I'm the one who taught her how to ride a bike, how to deal with a bully (strike fierce and fast), and how to incapacitate a guy when necessary. I didn't even know she was seeing anyone serious, and it's not for lack of communication. She texts me all the frigging time. Not a peep about this loser she was seeing. *Married?*

"It was a secret elopement," she says softly. "I was going to tell everyone later."

"And…"

"He got cold feet. Oh, Wyatt, it was so humiliating to be standing there in my wedding gown at our favorite restaurant. He knew the owner—" Her voice chokes, and she breaks down in tears.

My jaw clenches. *I will rip him limb from limb.*

I scoot my chair closer and stroke her hair back out of her face. "What's the guy's name?"

She meets my eyes, sniffling. "What?"

"I said what's his name? I will track him down like the dog he is and kick his ass." I turn to Snowball. "No offense to your kind. You have better breeding."

Snowball blinks her agreement from Kayla's arms.

"No, don't do that," Kayla says, horror laced in her voice. "I don't want him to know I care that much."

"Obviously you cared. You were about to shackle yourself to the guy for life. A guy I've never met, by the way. Don't *ever* do that again. Your family wants to be there." My voice strangles for a moment, and I cough to clear it. "I'm supposed to walk you down the aisle."

"I'm sorry. It seemed so romantic, the secret elopement wedding on New Year's Eve." She sets Snowball down to hug me.

After she settles in her seat again, I go back to my mission of tracking down the guy who hurt my baby sister. "Was it Christina's older brother? What's his name? Rick?" Christina is her best friend from home, now married with a baby.

"No! I never thought of Rick that way."

"Who introduced you to Mr. Cold Feet? Whose idea was it to have a secret elopement? How long were you seeing him? I have questions, Kayla." I tap the table for emphasis.

"You don't know him, okay? I met him online in *Always Summer*." That's a multiplayer role-playing game she likes.

I groan. "Didn't I tell you not to trust someone hiding behind a character online?"

She pouts. "He seemed different. Besides, we had a two-month in-person relationship, and we had stuff in common."

"Like what?"

She lifts her chin. "Like we both like *Always Summer*, Italian food, and he goes to my school." Her lower lip wobbles, and my chest tightens in sympathy. "It's not like it wasn't anything real." She drops her head in her hands.

I grind my teeth. How many times have I warned my sisters that the anonymity of the internet makes it a dangerous place? I should know. I've been working on online apps and tech since I was in high school. Wait a minute, I now have an important piece of information—he's a student at her university. Most likely a graduate student if he wanted to get married.

Kayla lifts her head, giving me the puppy eyes. *Ah, hell. I can never deny the puppy eyes.* "Can I stay with you for a bit? I just need a change of scenery."

She's living at home while finishing her master's thesis in biostatistics. Snoozefest to me, but I hear there's good prospects for her future career.

I gesture around us. "I didn't buy furniture yet except for the kitchen. All I have is one bed." *And that's where I sleep.* I left my stuff in storage while renovating. I need to get more furniture too since this house is so much bigger than my previous penthouse apartment.

She looks down at Snowball, as if she might have the right answer, and then lifts her gaze to me. "Please. I'll sleep on the floor. Mom will fuss too much over me, and I just need a break from everything that reminds me of..." She catches herself, keeping the loser's name to herself. I'll find out.

Still, she came to me. Not our sisters or her best friend. She needs *me*.

I cave. Not that I ever seriously considered turning her away. I only mentioned it's mostly empty to warn her it's not going to be luxurious like my apartment in the city. "You can have my room. I'll sleep on the sofa." There's a sofa in my empty dining room. It's where I spend most of my time.

"Thank you! You're the best brother in the world!" She kisses my cheek and gives me a squeeze.

"Yeah, yeah."

She lets go of me and rushes from the room. Snowball trots after her, tail wagging for the fun race.

I scoop the dog up as Kayla opens the front door and heads toward her Jeep. I watch for a moment as she opens the back and hauls out two huge suitcases. Looks like we both knew there was never a question of her staying here.

I set Snowball down, grab my boots, and order her to stay, shutting the door behind me. I meet Kayla in the driveway, taking the suitcases from her.

"Thanks," she says.

I grunt and head back in the house, ordering Snowball to back away from the door. Last thing I need is to lose Snowball in a snowdrift. Ha. Kayla follows me upstairs to my room, where there's just my duffel bags and a queen-sized bed on the metal frame it came with. This will eventually be a guest room.

She sits on the edge of the unmade bed, and I shoo her off. "You can have half the closet." I strip the bed and remake it with fresh sheets while she hangs up clothes in the closet.

After I finish making the bed, I grab one of the pillows for myself. I'm six feet two, so I doubt I'll fit comfortably on the sofa, but it's just until she's on her feet again. She needs a safe retreat to heal.

"I'm going to take a nap," she says, already getting into bed. "I only slept two hours last night."

I turn back, smooth her hair from her temple, and kiss the spot. "Sleep well, runt. I want a name when you wake up." I've had enough sisterly experience to know it's better to be up front with what needs to happen than try stuff behind their back. The scream of a banshee comes to mind. Though, sometimes, you just have to endure the wrath when shit needs to get done. I'm a fixer. It's what I do.

"Stop," she mumbles, curling up on her side.

I leave, shutting the door quietly behind me. Snowball's sitting there in the hallway, looking up at me expectantly. "I'll get your bed after she's done her nap. And don't even think of taking my pillow."

I exhale sharply. That guy took advantage of a trusting young woman, and when I find out who it is, he will pay.

4

Sydney

I shut my laptop and pace the hallway of my apartment, agitated by the truth of my financial situation. Last night's fundraiser only gave me enough to make this month's debt payment for the restaurant. It put off foreclosure, which I desperately needed, but I'd hoped for *at least* two months' worth of payments for some breathing room. I'll still have the same problem next month and the month after that, on and on. The hard truth is, it was a patch job for what will take a long time to fix.

When I first took over the restaurant, I managed to consolidate my father's debt into one loan. But I missed the last three payments, and if I miss any more, they'll start the foreclosure process. The threat of foreclosure keeps me up at night. I'll not only lose my family's legacy, I'll be homeless. I live in an apartment above the restaurant. Desperation claws at me, and I fight to keep a level head. I can't let that cloud my thinking.

I have only a few options—declare bankruptcy and shut the place down, sell it, or ask Harper or Wyatt for a loan. I can't bear to shut it down. I'm the fourth generation of proud Robinsons running the place. It can't die on my watch.

It's my own fault for taking on what Drew told me was a

losing proposition. He wanted to sell; I wanted to hold on to our family's legacy. The whole town's legacy, really. If I sell, it could be demolished and turned into a parking lot or a bank or a gas station. Something shitty like that. If I could even find a buyer in the dead of winter. Real estate's gone up around here, but that's mostly housing. This place is old and not zoned residential. It would be a long shot.

Harper's offered to give me a loan, but here's the thing. Ever since she became a famous actress, people have been taking advantage of her sweet, generous nature. She complains bitterly about it. I never want her to think of me like that. Plus, she's pregnant, getting married, and just bought an expensive house. And she spends generously to take care of her elderly grandmother, who lives alone. It feels wrong to add to Harper's burden, and I don't want to risk our friendship.

I stop pacing, look to the ceiling, and blow out a breath. Wyatt. He's got loads of money, knows my place is in trouble, and has taken an interest in it. Not the good kind of interest, more like the critical kind. I press my lips together. I need to put my irritation aside and approach him in a calm, cool, professional manner.

Can I do it? Can I deal with his smirks and criticisms, put all that aside, and work with him?

Or will I end up throttling him?

I may need serious stress therapy after this. Not that I don't already have a ton of stress. I should research more about him and his business dealings. See what I'm dealing with here. I loosen my clenched jaw. Harper likes him. I cling to that thought. He can't be one hundred percent awful, right?

The man's been invading my dreams for weeks, those whisky eyes smoldering at me. It's so embarrassing. How can I be both irritated and attracted at the same time? It's messing with my head. I need to chill if I want to have a chance of working with him professionally. No more dirty dreams, no more temper.

I'm saved from further angst by a text from Jenna. My

friends are here. I head downstairs to let them in the front door of the restaurant. It's closed for New Year's Day, but we're getting together at the bar for our last Thursday Night Wine Club just the three of us since next Thursday starts ladies' night.

Once we're settled at the bar with our wine, I lift my glass of merlot and clink it against Jenna's and Audrey's. "To the Thursday Night Wine Club."

Audrey purses her lips, looking very much the prim librarian. She's not prim, exactly, but she is a librarian. Her black floral blouse with a white Peter Pan collar combined with her bun held together by a couple of pencils adds to the effect. She spent today restoring order to the Summerdale Library's shelves. *On her day off.* "It was supposed to be a book club," she says in an aggrieved tone, holding up a book written by some guy I never heard of. "Thursday Night *Book* Club."

"Seriously, Aud, who were we kidding?" I say with a laugh. "All we did was talk and drink wine. I gave it a name that reflects what we actually do."

"I tried to bring the conversation back to the book," she retorts.

Jenna leans forward, tucking a lock of blond hair behind her ear. She's in a cute white sweater with a lacy front and jeans. Only Jenna could wear white and never worry about spilling anything on it. "Book club would probably work better at the library."

Audrey brightens. "I could get one started. When's good for you both?"

Jenna crinkles her nose. "I like meeting here. Besides, you never let us eat at the library."

"It's just to protect the books," Audrey says. "It could still be fun. I'll serve wine too as long as it's not red."

"I only read horror," I say. "Sorry. I know you like the latest hot literary book."

"I could read horror," Audrey offers.

I shoot her a look. "Sweetie, you had nightmares for two years after we watched *Carrie*."

"I did not."

Jenna chimes in. "And you made us watch only comedies at sleepovers forever after."

Audrey huffs. "I'm twenty-eight. I can handle Stephen King now. We were eleven when we watched *Carrie*. That's a very impressionable age."

I go behind the bar for some pretzels and pour them in a bowl. "Why don't you start a book club, and then see who else in town enjoys books that you like? Wouldn't it be better to talk about the book with someone who appreciates it?"

Audrey wags her finger. "I'm not giving up on you ladies."

I set the pretzels on the bar and join them again. "Anyway, with half-price drinks, I'm hoping it'll be packed. Get the word out to everyone you know. I'm doing the flyer-in-the-mailbox thing again. It brought out people for New Year's. Hopefully, single guys will show up to meet all the ladies. There have to be some bachelors in the area, right? I'll post the flyers in nearby towns too."

Jenna sighs. "That's the one thing I miss. Summerdale is mostly families and some empty nesters who haven't moved to Florida yet for retirement."

"There's our newest eligible bachelor, Wyatt Winters," Audrey says in a teasing tone.

Billionaire business guru with a devilish smile and a soul to match.

Yet I'm actually considering swallowing my pride to talk to him about saving this place.

Desperate times.

"Handsome as sin," Jenna says dreamily.

I stiffen. *Is Jenna interested in him?*

Not that it matters to me personally. I just don't want one of my best friends to be with Satan. Wart. Whatever. He's good at business, but that doesn't mean he'd be a good boyfriend. He'd probably criticize constantly. Nope. Jenna should stay away.

Jenna continues. "Poor guy in that big house by himself. I should bring him a housewarming gift from my bakery.

Maybe an assortment of cookies, or do you think cupcakes would be better?"

"Have you seen his ass in those jeans?" Audrey whispers. "I doubt he eats many sweets."

"Never noticed," I lie. "But you both should stay away. All he does is criticize my place, and I bet he does the same thing to everyone in his life." I shove a pretzel in my mouth so I can't spew anything further about the man I've been desperately trying not to think so much about.

Jenna and Audrey exchange a look.

"What?" I snap, wineglass halfway to my mouth.

"Nothing," Audrey says.

Jenna nudges my side. "Wyatt's not the only bachelor in town. You have single brothers who might be looking to meet someone."

"Ha! They might be prowling, there's a difference. Anyway, I'm not running a ladies' night so my brothers can find hookups. Let's talk about something else."

Audrey nods enthusiastically. "Did either of you read *Disappear Me*?"

"Sure, I read the title," I say, pointing to her book. "It's missing some letters."

"Because you're supposed to be imagining them disappearing!" she huffs.

I grin. "Joking. What's got you so tense? Did something happen with Drew?"

"No, nothing," Audrey lies, reaching to twirl a lock of hair that's not there because her hair is pulled back in a bun. I know her tells. Every hair twirl is a comfort from the guilt over her lie.

"You can tell us," Jenna says gently.

"There's nothing to tell!" Audrey exclaims.

We both stare at her. She's never excitable. Steady as she goes, that's our Audrey.

"Okay," Jenna says quietly.

Audrey jabs a finger at me. "You slapped your ass at Wyatt and gave him the finger. So what's going on there?"

"Sounds like a Sydney mating ritual," Jenna quips.

They laugh, and the tension is broken. I don't mind if it makes Audrey feel better. It must suck to worship a guy from afar. I told Audrey to try online dating, but she's too afraid of meeting up with a creep. Jenna and I used to live in Brooklyn and Hoboken respectively before we moved back home, and both places had decent dating scenes. Not that anything worked out. Jenna only wanted casual, feeling like she wanted to meet lots of different people. Me, I had a couple of relationships that lasted for a year. There's something comforting about having someone to go out with for every occasion. Until you don't. That's the hard part.

Jenna grabs a handful of pretzels. "Gotta say, Syd, it's not wise to piss off the billionaire guy who's known for philanthropy. Harper told us the deal with Wyatt last night."

"And isn't he a business genius?" Audrey asks.

Even though I'm considering approaching Wyatt, it would only be for a loan that I paid back with interest.

I scowl. "I'm not a charity case. He can donate his billions to some worthy organization like Best Friends Care." That's a nonprofit that Harper supports in a big way. They train shelter animals as service dogs for people with disabilities that show and some that don't. They help a lot of military veterans with PTSD. Sometimes I wonder if my brother Drew, a former Army Ranger, could benefit from something like that. He's so stoic and on the grumpy side, though he's always been that way. He should get a dog or two. He has a house with a yard.

Jenna keeps pressing on the Wyatt button. "I'm sure Wyatt's already donated to them since he's friends with Harper, but maybe—"

I set my glass down harder than I mean to, nearly toppling it. "Can we talk about anything else besides Wyatt's billions?"

Audrey's eyes widen. "Little worked up there, lady. Maybe you could work out a loan as a friend of a friend? You know, because of the Harper connection." At my silence, she adds, "If you could find a way to be a teensy bit more friendly to him."

I gesture wildly, pissed all over again about the man. "He

criticizes everything about this place! He even suggested we get a new name!"

"It *is* kind of a weird name," Jenna says. "What's a horseman anyway?"

I huff. "A stagecoach guy? I don't know! The point is it's historic."

Audrey lifts a finger. "A horseman is a man who really likes horses."

"Half man, half horse," Jenna declares as if that's the final word on horseman.

Audrey tilts her head. "Isn't that a centaur?"

"Anyway—" I start.

"And the inn part doesn't fit either," Audrey points out. "Now it's just a restaurant."

I throw my hands up. "It's the centerpiece of town! A legacy I need to protect, okay?"

Jenna and Audrey exchange another look.

"Are you okay?" Audrey asks.

"I'm fine." I go for my wine and toss back the rest. "Sorry I snapped at you. I'm just in a tight spot right now, but I'll figure it out."

"The New Year's fundraiser wasn't a success?" Audrey asks.

"It was, but..." I sigh. "I only made enough for this month's debt payment, and I can't have a fundraiser every month. I just don't know how much longer I can keep going like this."

Audrey squeezes my arm. "Oh, Syd, I'm so sorry."

Jenna presses her lips together. "How bad is it?"

"I really don't want to talk about it." I'm embarrassed at how far into debt my father put this place. He operated at a loss for years and just kept racking up credit cards, second mortgages, and high-interest loans to keep things going. He didn't want to be a failure in our family business and didn't want to burden his children. My brothers and I had moved on to other vocations. I was working for a boutique advertising agency, my youngest brother Caleb is a model, Drew runs his own dojo in town, Eli's a cop, and Adam is a master carpenter. Then our dad gave The Horseman Inn to the oldest, Drew, in his will.

Drew ran it for six months—basically working two full-time jobs—declared it a money pit and asked us if we'd be okay with him selling it. That's when I jumped in, moving back home to protect our family legacy. I was so confident with the right marketing I could get this place going again. Turns out you need more than marketing savvy in this situation. You need money.

"Come on," Jenna says. "It's us. How bad is it?"

"Bad," I say.

Jenna gives me a small shove. "Would you stop being the stoic tough one for one minute and tell us?"

"I'm not stoic and tough," I say. "That's Drew."

Audrey chugs her wine.

"You're the female version," Jenna says. "You always want to shoulder the burden on your own."

Like my dad. "An admirable quality."

"But sometimes you have to let your friends help," Jenna says.

"You'll feel better if you share," Audrey says.

I exhale sharply, taking in the two women I've known since we were young girls. These are my ride-or-die friends. I'd do anything for them. But I won't bring them down with me. "If I miss another payment, they'll start the foreclosure process. I've already missed three in a row. Every month is so stressful, not knowing if I can scrape together the payment."

"Oh, Sydney," Audrey says softly.

"So sorry," Jenna says.

I put some enthusiasm into my voice. "It's not over yet. There's still a chance that ladies' night and Friday trivia night can get us back on track. It'll make this place more of a community hangout. I think the key is to give people a reason to be here and keep returning. And a lot of people have off for the holidays, probably getting antsy at home. I have a good feeling there'll be a crowd tomorrow for trivia night."

I don't say a word about possibly turning to Wyatt. I need

to research his business dealings and take a big dose of *suck it up* before approaching him.

Jenna and Audrey exchange a worried look.

"What's the full amount you need?" Jenna asks.

An impossible number. An embarrassing number.

I shake my head. "It'll turn around, I know it. It's a new year, ladies."

My friends shoot me worried looks. Yeah, I'm having trouble believing it too.

5

Sydney

It's the day after New Year's, which means it's our first Friday trivia night. I'm running half-price appetizers before seven, hoping to attract more people. Trivia starts at six at the bar. Drinks are our big moneymaker. Fingers crossed that people will linger afterwards for dinner. It's not just about putting money into the coffers—though obviously I need that—it's about making The Horseman Inn more of a community hangout.

By the time we get started at six, I'm pleased to see we've got thirteen people here to play. All locals—teachers, mostly, as well as the ladies who showed up to meet Harper on New Year's. I think they have a knitting club because they're all knitting something while pausing to sip their margaritas and answer questions.

I'm the emcee, working to keep the energy up and people interested. I even skipped the usual staff T-shirt in favor of a white T-shirt with a rhinestone question mark I bedazzled myself. Black skinny jeans and my black high-heeled boots complete the emcee ensemble. I'd hoped to score some question-mark earrings, but no one I knew had a pair I could borrow. I'm doing this on the cheap, which means I came up with all the questions, made a little slideshow on my laptop to display the questions on the TVs over the bar, and they're writing the answers on old-fashioned pen and paper. Five rounds of trivia. The prize is a gaudy huge gold medal necklace (fake), and everyone gets five-dollar coupons to use on their next visit. I also declared today Fajita Friday, so they'll think of ordering fajitas, nachos, and margaritas.

The questions are all over the place, some easy, some near impossible, except for the biggest factoid-storing eggheads out there. For example: on an internet browser, what does www stand for (World Wide Web. Easy.) In Greek mythology, who was the first woman on earth? (Pandora. Difficult.)

Everyone's gathered at the bar. My friends are here, too, which gives us three teams of five. We're just getting to the second round when I see our hostess seat Wyatt and a beautiful brunette at a corner table in the back room across from us. I still, a sudden coldness hitting me. I didn't know he had a girlfriend.

I can't seem to look away. He pulls the chair out for his date before taking the seat across from her, smiling and saying something that doesn't look remotely smirky. I guess he has good manners for *some* people.

He must be into her because he doesn't even glance this way. I thought he lived to harass me. Who is she?

"Syd?" Betsy, my bartender, asks. She's in her twenties with pink hair, multiple piercings, and a unique style that's part retro fifties' and part embellished modern wear. Today's outfit is a cute fuzzy peach sweater with cropped black pants sporting sequined daisies. "You want me to do the remote for the next question?"

I stare at the remote in my hand. I forgot I was holding it. *Focus!* "I got it." I turn and press the button for the next question, which I read out loud with enthusiasm. "What country consumes the most chocolate per capita?"

The crowd erupts in discussion. Since there's only two guys here, high school teachers, it's mostly the women enthusiastically discussing chocolate and what kind they like best.

"Write it down, everyone!" I yell above the chatter. "It's still anyone's game!"

They quiet down, and I press a sound effect on my phone for a playful countdown.

Jenna gestures me closer across the bar.

I lean in.

Her green eyes twinkle as she whispers, "I spot Satan with an angel."

I keep my eyes on her, resisting the impulse to look again. "Oh, yeah? I hadn't noticed."

She rolls her eyes. "Right." She leans in. "So now that you don't have to worry he'll get the wrong idea, maybe you could make nice with him."

"I was never concerned about that." The attraction has been humiliatingly one-sided and completely involuntary. I smile serenely, doing my best impression of a saint. "Besides, I'm nice to everyone. I'm Miss Hospitality."

She cocks her head. "Then go over there and say hello with your big bright smile of welcome. It's a new year, good for a fresh start. A *much-needed* one."

I narrow my eyes. I'm not hitting him up for money in front of his date. Besides, I did some research on him today, and I have serious concerns about the way he operates. He invests and turns around failing businesses, yes, but he also keeps control as a partner. I can't give up a piece of my restaurant. This place has been fully owned by a Robinson for generations. No outsiders.

"I'm hosting, Jenna. Get back to game play, please."

She turns and waves at him. "Hi, Wyatt!"

My cheeks flush. I have no idea why. It's not like he's watching me. He's with someone. I busy myself tucking glasses away under the bar.

"Hey," he calls over. I'm not sure he knows her name. He certainly can't remember mine, always calling me Cindy. Irritating man.

"That wasn't so hard," Jenna says to me smugly.

Audrey waves at him too.

I steadfastly avoid looking for a good ten seconds. Finally, I risk a glance over. He's deep in conversation with his mystery woman. She's not local. Is she visiting from the city? Not that I need to know. Just idle curiosity.

By the time the trivia game wraps up—the elementary school teacher team is enthusiastically snapping photos with their gold medal—I decide a friendly hello to the patrons in the back room is in order. There's a family there now, along with Wyatt and his girlfriend. This is what good restaurant owners do.

I stop at the family's table first. I haven't seen them here before. "Hi, I'm Sydney, the manager, how's everything going tonight?"

The mom smiles. "Good, thanks. We just moved to town. First time trying it."

The dad nods as he chews, and their three kids are too busy eating their burgers to look up.

I smile. "Well, welcome to Summerdale. I hope to see you back."

I turn toward Wyatt's table just as he's standing, his brow furrowed with concern as he puts his arm around his girlfriend's shoulders and guides her out. She's crying.

"Excuse us," he says as he passes me. "I left enough to cover the bill."

I follow a few steps behind, watching them go. I don't think they had a fight or broke up because she wouldn't want him touching her. He guides her through the front dining room, opens the door for her, and then they're gone.

I'm not going to spy on them. Not my business.

I make my way to the front dining room, just doing my job, checking if everyone's happy with their meal. There's two tables with couples deep in conversation. Probably date night out for the parents. I glance toward the parking lot, but it's too dark to see.

He seemed kind of concerned and caring. The complete opposite of the way he is with me. I exhale sharply and push him to the back of my mind.

Where he lingers for the rest of the night. Dammit.

A week later, Harper's back in town. To see her two weeks in a row is a surprise, but I'm happy. She and Garrett just showed up at The Horseman Inn for lunch.

I meet them in the front dining room, where they've been seated. Harper stands to hug me. "Are you trying to single-handedly keep this place in business?" I whisper jokingly.

She smiles and pulls back, holding my arms. "The food's so good I told Garrett we had to drive out here for lunch." She says it extra loud for the benefit of our Saturday lunch crowd. All three tables full.

Truth is, most of our profit is in the bar, but I want to keep this a family place too. It's important for the whole community to feel welcome here.

Garrett stands to greet me, and I give him a hug too. He's like a big muscled teddy bear despite his tough-looking exterior. His dark brown hair is clipped short, emphasizing the sharp angles of his cheekbones and square jaw.

"Taking good care of our girl?" I ask, socking him on the shoulder.

"Sure am, and vice versa."

They take their seats again.

"Sit with us for a few minutes," Harper urges.

I take the chair next to her. "No guard today?" Usually Harper's bodyguard sticks close.

"I don't worry so much about security here, but he is with us," she says. "We left him at my grandmother's house. They're watching an old cowboy movie."

"Really?" My mind conjures her cantankerous eighty-seven-year-old grandmother sitting in her old high-back chair, while across from her, big muscled Joe with his neck tattoo sits on her plastic slip-covered floral sofa. An unusual pairing.

"Yeah," Harper says. "Once Garrett told her Joe was cool, she gave him a chance. Garrett can do no wrong in her eyes."

"Aren't you special?" I ask him.

He lifts a massive shoulder. "What can I say? Chicks dig me."

I laugh. "So will you guys be around a while? I could check if Jenna and Audrey can meet up with us."

"Sure, that'd be great," Harper says. "After lunch, we're heading over to Wyatt's place to check out the renovation. You want to come along?"

"He invited you over?" I blurt. Stupid question. Of course he invited them. They wouldn't just show up, driving all the way out here from the city.

Harper's brows lift. "Yeah, he wants Garrett to check on the progress and give his opinion on stuff. He's like an expert on every aspect of construction." She smiles at him, hearts in her eyes, and he brushes a kiss over her knuckles. Her lips part, and it looks like a kiss is about to happen.

I turn away, feeling like I'm intruding on a personal moment. "So, I should—"

"I just can't wait to see the inside of the place," Harper says. "Aren't you dying of curiosity? Remember how scared we were of that old house growing up? No one ever went trick-or-treating there." She turns to Garrett. "We thought it was haunted."

"Naturally," he says. "Big empty house on top of the hill with a lighthouse on dry land. What else could it be?"

Harper nods once and continues. "People said that the old man who used to live there was nuts, building that lighthouse. You've got to come with us, Syd. We'll finally see what all the fuss was about."

My heart pounds. *What is wrong with me?* It's not like I'm afraid of ghosts. Why does every part of me want to scream no? It's that woman. I don't want to witness more of Wyatt with his beautiful girlfriend, all kindness and caring. Everything he's not with me.

Am I actually jealous? Hell no. It just rubs me the wrong way because he goes out of his way to antagonize me.

"I don't know if I can get away," I say, gesturing around us. "Lots of work to do."

"He told us to stop by any time," Harper says. "We can go late afternoon. Don't you close for a few hours between lunch and dinner?" This is true. There's a gap in shifts and two hours of dead time.

I blink, the walls closing in on me. "Yes, but there's still work to do."

"Oh, Syd, are you still fighting with him?" she asks.

Like it's my fault? Wart is the one who nonstop criticizes everything around here. He can't even remember my name! It's not that difficult. I work hard to sound calm. "No. I was never fighting with him." *He antagonizes me, and I respond in kind.*

She exchanges a look with Garrett before turning back to me. "This might be a good opportunity to mend fences, you know? Meet him on his home turf, find something nice to say about his place, and you're on the first step to the road of…friendship."

My head snaps toward her, instantly suspicious. "Why did you pause there?"

"Pause where?" she asks innocently.

She's a fantastic actress, but I know her too well for that. "Before friendship."

She leans close. "It's no secret that tension between a man and a woman is often…" She mouths *sexual.*

I fight back a blush. *All those sexy dreams.* "Nope. That's *not* what's going on here. Besides, he has a girlfriend. I saw her last week."

"Oh, I didn't know that." She turns to Garrett. "Did you know?"

"No, but guys don't share as much by text as you women do."

"What exactly did he say in his text?" Harper asks.

Garrett shrugs. "He said come up and see the place, and I said, okay, when? No further sharing happened. Other than some renovation stuff."

Harper smiles, grabs him by the shirt, and pulls him close for a kiss. "I just love how you get it, honey."

I look away. Harper is not normally mushy like this. She was raised by her tough grandmother. This is what love does to a person. Makes them completely unaware of how ridiculous they sound. Not me. I've been in love before, and not once have I been as ridiculously mushy as she is.

I clear my throat. "I'll, uh, text Jenna and Audrey. Maybe they'd like to see the old place." I send a text through our group text and stand. "Back to work for me. I'll let you know if I hear from them." My phone chimes, and I check the screen. "They hit the mall for the January sales."

"Bummer," Harper says. "At least we've got you. Maybe they'll be done by late afternoon, and we can all go to Wyatt's place together."

"Why does everyone have to go see Wyatt?" I ask with more bite than I intended. It just feels like everyone and everything is pulling me toward the one man on earth who makes me nuts.

Her eyes widen. "I just thought it would be cool to see the haunted house we were terrified of as kids together. What's your problem with Wyatt?"

I clench my teeth. "I don't have a problem with Wyatt." Except that my friends keep pushing me to make nice with him. It's as if everyone's forgotten how much he's insulted me and my place, all with a smirk on his face. He knows very well what he's doing. Even ignoring all that, I'm not sure I can work with him, given how he takes a piece of every business he invests in. Unfortunately, I still need to consider approaching him, but I'm not ready to do that until I can figure out a deal that leaves me as full owner of my restaurant. I'm just not sure what I can offer that he'd want.

Everything with Wyatt is so damn difficult. The man knocks me off balance in every way, which is why I'm not ready to visit him and "make nice."

"Mmm-hmm," she says. "Tension." But she says it like *sexual*.

My cheeks heat, and I quickly turn away to hide it, waving over my shoulder as I go back to work.

How did I get conned into this? I'm sitting in the back seat of Harper's black Mercedes SUV with Jenna and Audrey on our way to Wyatt's place. Audrey's in the middle seat because she's the smallest.

Adrenaline races through me as the car makes its way up the winding hill to his house. It's a large two-story with gray clapboard siding. The gray lighthouse with a white top is to the right of the house. I stare at the lighthouse. *Why?*

"I only have an hour before I have to get back," I say.

"We know," a chorus of voices returns.

"The place is mostly empty," Garrett says from the driver's seat. "We're just going to take the tour. I doubt he even has anywhere for us to sit."

"Aren't you guys dying of curiosity?" Harper asks with an enthusiastic smile at those of us trapped in the back seat.

"Yes," Audrey says.

"Totally," Jenna says.

I'm so tense I'm about to leap out of the vehicle.

"Syd?" Harper asks.

"Yes, of course I'm curious. That's the only reason I'm here." I stare out the tinted window. *Almost there.*

"Syd and Wyatt have a thing," Jenna says.

My head snaps to her. "We do not have a thing."

"You kinda do," Audrey says.

"It's sexual tension," Harper says matter-of-factly.

"He has a girlfriend!" I exclaim.

My friends titter.

"Syd has a huge buildup of tension," Jenna says. "It's been what…" She starts counting on her fingers.

Months. Too many months.

I glare at her. "Would you shut up? Garrett doesn't want to hear about my sex life."

He grins. "Pretend I'm not here."

"Six months!" Jenna crows. "Right? Since Todd."

Todd was the guy I briefly dated when I lived in Hoboken before I came home to take over the restaurant. And I'm not going to share that it never got that far. I tried, I really did. But he touched me so gently, with barely there feather-like touches, I felt like I was with a girl. I need a man who's not afraid to grab on and take. That's how I am. I probably scared Todd away with my boldness. So, yeah, it's been more than six months. Whatever. There's more important things in life than sex.

I'm just so sick of crappy lovers. At my age I know what I like and don't like, and why is that so hard for a guy to get? I'm tired of directing—*harder, no, not there, here. More of that, a little to the right.*

It's a basic problem of incompatibility for the most part. It's not me.

The car comes to a halt alongside a red Jeep. There's also a silver BMW SUV. I bet his girlfriend's here. Welp, he must've made her feel better after she cried, or she wouldn't have stuck around. I force myself to take a deep breath over the tightness in my chest. It doesn't make sense to feel hurt. So he's a beast to me and a sweetheart to her. Why do I even care what he does?

I get out of the car and shove my hands in the pockets of my black down coat. The faint sound of a dog barking catches my attention. There it is, by the front window. A little white shih tzu with its front paws on the windowsill, barking like it means business. Must be his girlfriend's dog. I imagine Wyatt would have a big tough-looking dog like my brother Adam's bulldog.

Garrett reaches the blue front door first, and we all gather behind him. I spot Wyatt scooping up the dog before walking toward the door.

I slip to the back of the group, standing behind tall Jenna.

"Hiding?" she asks.

I don't respond. I don't know why I want a buffer. I don't know why my pulse is racing and my mouth is dry. I must be coming down with something.

6

"Welcome to *Casa Winters*," Wyatt says when he answers the door.

I follow behind as everyone greets him warmly. I'm going to do the same, blend with the crowd. Just a warm hello. Or hi. Keep it simple.

But the moment we come face-to-face, his mouth curves up into a small smirk, his whisky eyes sparkling, and not one thing comes out of my mouth. Worse, my stomach flutters, actually flutters. It must be because those eyes feature in all my sexy dreams.

Damn you, Satan man!

He sets the little dog down, who immediately starts sniffing my boots. "Cindy, you made it. I didn't know if you ever left The Horseman Inn."

He's deliberately goading me with the Cindy, and I refuse to rise to the bait. "Yes, I do have a life."

"She's due back in an hour," Harper puts in helpfully.

"Thank you for the reminder, Harp," I say, my gaze locked on Wyatt in some kind of staring contest.

Wyatt blinks first. "Well then, let's get on with the tour." He gestures for us to follow, and then looks down at the dog. "Snowball, come."

Snowball? The dog obediently trots after Wyatt as he walks over to Garrett.

It has to be a shared couple dog. I can't imagine Wyatt would get a white shih tzu and name it something cutesy like Snowball. He's *Satan*. Not a snowball's chance in hell. I laugh to myself at my little joke.

I follow the group as Wyatt gestures around the living room just off the foyer. It's a large empty space with cream-colored walls and an ornate fireplace with a white carved wood mantel and surround. "We took out the dividing wall from what used to be a parlor and living room, so it's one large living room now. Under the tarps is original wide plank oak flooring. I plan to restore it."

Garrett goes over to inspect the fireplace.

The windows are tall and start low to the ground, letting in lots of light. I look around. I can see the potential as a modernized space. Everything's light and bright. There's no creepy haunted feeling either. I guess when you don't know what's up with a place, it's easy to make up a story. It wasn't just us kids who thought an eccentric old man used to live up here in a haunted house. Everyone talked about it like that in town.

"I'm going to put some cool chandeliers in here," Wyatt says from across the space.

"You need three," Garrett says. "Unless you add in additional lighting."

We continue on to a large modern kitchen with white cabinets, sleek light gray granite on the counters and the large center island, and stainless steel appliances. Across from the island is a large light wood kitchen table with matching wooden chairs with seat cushions. It's all surprisingly homey and not at all what I expected he'd have. How does Satan decorate hell? Ha-ha. Considering how old the house is, I thought it'd be drafty too. Even my feet are toasty warm.

"Did you put in heated floors?" I ask.

"Yup. Kitchen and bathroom," Wyatt replies. "Not hard to add when you're putting in new flooring."

I stare at him, and then realize I'm staring and belatedly

nod. It's just that he seems so different standing in this beautiful space. Relaxed and at home. *Well, duh, Syd! He is at home.*

"Right through here," he says, gesturing for us to follow him through an archway.

This next room has only a brown leather sofa. Another fireplace, less ornate than the first, and a hardwood floor with a few scratches. A pillow and blanket are folded neatly on one end of the sofa. Is this where he sleeps? Where does his girlfriend sleep? There's no way they both fit on that sofa. Wyatt's as big as my brothers, more than six feet and broad shouldered. His long-sleeved black cotton shirt seems to emphasize those wide shoulders and the curve of bicep. The black really brings out those whiskey eyes.

"I call this my sofa room, but it'll eventually be the dining room," he says.

Stop staring! He has a girlfriend. Not that it matters because, even if he was single and not irritating long enough for something to happen, I'm never crossing the line with someone I hope to have a professional relationship with.

"Next is the future library," he says, leading the way to the next room.

Audrey gets excited and dashes ahead to see. Our little bookworm.

I follow them. It's just an empty room, but it has a bay window deep enough to sit in and a fireplace. I could imagine curling up in a comfy chair to read on a rainy day.

"What's your plan?" Audrey asks Wyatt eagerly. She'll probably want to arrange all his books for him, and then stay to read as many as possible.

Wyatt gestures to the wall across the room. "Built-in bookcases with cabinets on the bottom for storage here." He gestures to the adjacent wall. "And here." His eyes meet mine suddenly, giving me a jolt.

He raises his brows, looking at me expectantly.

"Sorry, what?" I say when it seems I must've missed something.

One corner of his mouth quirks up. "I said the library is

part of what Adam will be working on." That's my brother, the master carpenter.

My mouth is so dry. I lick my lips. "Cool. I'm sure you'll be happy with his work."

"That's why I hired him."

I rub the side of my neck, looking away. It's the nicest thing he's ever said to me, complimenting my brother.

"This is so wonderful," Audrey says in a breathy voice. "A real library at home."

"The bay window will be a reading nook." Wyatt gestures toward it. "Shelves all the way to the ceiling, and a ladder on wheels to reach the high stuff."

Audrey claps, beaming and looking around. She especially would appreciate a rolling ladder since she's short at five feet one. "I can't wait to see it!"

Wyatt gives her a genuine nonsmirky smile, and my breath catches. That kind of smile lights up his face. "You're all welcome back for the grand reveal, which will hopefully be in March. So, back to my humble living space. Upstairs has nothing going on yet. There's one finished bathroom and, once we can get the permit cleared, I'm having a master bathroom and powder room installed. Can you believe this huge house only has one bathroom? Obviously the old guy didn't have daughters."

He says that like he knows all about women hogging the bathroom. Guess he's probably had a lot of experience with women. I bet they were all beautiful models like his girlfriend. *Whatever.* My younger brother Caleb is a model. No big deal.

We follow him back to the sofa room. "Have a seat," he says, gesturing to the sofa, where Snowball is curled on top of his pillow.

He scoops her up. "What did I tell you about my pillow? I'll get your bed." He turns to us. "Be right back."

Harper takes a seat on the sofa and gestures us over. Jenna and Audrey sit on either side of her, and I perch on the sofa arm on the opposite side from the pillow and blanket. I don't want to touch his sleeping things. Too personal.

Garrett wanders around the room, poking at the ceiling and inspecting the windows. Wyatt returns and sets a pink and white paw-print doggie bed in front of the fireplace. Then he sets Snowball in it, chucks her under the chin, and heads over to Garrett. Snowball curls up and resumes her nap.

"I can see the potential," Harper says to us. Wyatt and Garrett are across the room, deep into renovation talk.

"It's going to be beautiful," Audrey says.

"I can't wait to see it when it's done," Jenna says.

"I don't know why he comes into my restaurant so much," I say. "He has a gourmet kitchen right here. Did you see the stove has six burners?"

Jenna laughs. "Gee, I can't imagine why he goes to your restaurant so much."

My friends titter. *He has a girlfriend!*

"He must be a terrible cook," I say. "Now that his girlfriend's in town, I haven't seen him much. Maybe she's cooking."

And then she walks into the room, holding a laptop to her chest. She's early twenties with dark brown hair that falls in a glossy wave to her shoulders, big brown eyes, delicate cheekbones, a cute doll-like mouth that's sort of plump and pursed. She's dressed casually in a pale pink tunic over black leggings with pink fuzzy socks.

She smiles at us. "Hi, everyone. I'm Kayla."

We all say hello. I watch as she hands over the laptop to Wyatt.

"Did you enjoy your chick flick?" he asks, tucking it under one arm.

She smiles. "Yes. I cried at the end."

"Of course you did." He looks at her feet. "Go put on shoes. I don't want you stepping on a loose nail or getting a splinter."

She obediently turns and walks out of the room, presumably for her shoes. Wow. I certainly wouldn't tolerate my guy ordering me around like that.

He flips open the laptop lid and walks over to the entrance

of the room, yelling toward the ceiling. "And bring the charging cord, please!"

Well, at least he added a please at the end. Reminds me of my older brother Drew barking out orders military style.

"Wyatt, you ever been in the military?" I ask.

He turns. "No. Why?"

Because you order your girlfriend around. "No reason."

He walks over to me, a small smirk on his gorgeous face. "Come on, Cindy, tell me why you asked. Do I sound like a drill sergeant?"

The room goes silent. I can feel my friends' stares, probably anticipating I'm going to fight with him. No, I can be civil despite the smirk I'm desperate to smack off his face. And the fact that he purposely called me Cindy just to irk me.

"Actually, yes," I say evenly. "You just ordered your girlfriend to put on shoes."

He makes a face, looking at me like I have two heads. "Gross. She's not my girlfriend. She's my baby sister."

My pulse shoots up. *He's single.*

"What made you think she was my girlfriend?" he asks.

"I saw you with your arm around her at my restaurant." I glance around for confirmation, but my friends look like they're just enjoying the show. *Should I pass out the popcorn?*

He looks to the ceiling and blows out a breath before leveling an affronted look on me. "I had my arm around her because she was about to have a public meltdown. Some things are private, Sydney."

He said my name. No Cindy to irk me. And he's a protective big brother. I respect that.

I was lucky to have two awesome big brothers looking out for me when I was a kid. How else would I have made it through my teen years after Mom died? Drew and Adam taught me everything I needed to know, which boils down to *be proud to be a Robinson* and *stand your ground.* They expected me to be strong and speak my mind, even when riddled with teenaged insecurities. And I did, even though I sometimes wanted to hide. They set a good example too.

"That's why you're sleeping on the sofa," I say quietly,

thinking of the sacrifice he made for his younger sister. She must have his room.

He rubs the back of his neck. "Yeah, she just needs a break."

I want to ask why, but it seems too nosy to ask.

Then he shocks me, sharing more about his sister all on his own. "Right now she's in a vulnerable state." His jaw tightens, and he glances behind him, checking if she's there. He turns back to me. "She's heartbroken, and when I finally get a name out of her, I'm going to make that guy's life a living hell."

My lips part in surprise. Taking his sister in, kicking ass on her behalf. He's *kind*.

I sock him on the shoulder. "You're a good big brother."

"Why do you sound so surprised? And *ow*." He rubs his shoulder.

I shrug.

He shakes his head and looks over at Snowball. He has a little white dog named Snowball. How adorable is that?

"I think it's great," I offer.

He looks back at me, one corner of his mouth turning up.

I find myself smiling. Then I realize everyone is looking at us and smiling. I drop the smile. The last thing I need is to hear all about how I have hearts in my eyes for Wyatt Winters on the drive home.

I don't.

But I may have misjudged him.

7

———

Mondays are my day off from The Horseman Inn. It's afternoon when I finally catch up on paperwork and move money around to keep our suppliers happy and staff paid.

My phone blares with a severe weather alert that reminds me we're expecting a major snowstorm, nine to twelve inches of snowfall with gusting winds. Crap. I hope we don't lose power. It happens regularly around here when downed trees take out wires, and that means I have to close the restaurant until the power is restored, which can take days. I have a backup generator that keeps the refrigerator and freezers going, but it's not powerful enough for all the cooking and other essentials needed to stay open. Besides, most people won't venture out until the roads are cleared of trees and downed wires. I'd better make a run to the grocery store for some essentials.

It's just a short walk to the small grocery in town, so I put on my black down coat, gray knit cap, and snow boots. When I get there, the store isn't crowded. Most people stocked up this weekend, but I was working then.

The shopkeeper, Nicholas, looks the same as always—like Santa. He's an older man with white hair, a long beard, and a potbelly. And he's got the name, like St. Nicholas. He plays Santa at the annual holiday pancake breakfast. When I was a kid, I was in awe that I could see Santa year-round, though he explained he was just Santa's helper.

"Hi, Nicholas," I say.

"Hello, Sydney. I'm shutting down in half an hour, so you made it just in time. Have to get home before the storm."

"I won't be long." I make my way to the refrigerated section in the back of the store in search of milk and cookie dough. After I find those essential items, I take a look around for anything I might've missed. I have bread, but you know what I don't have? Ice cream. I could make chocolate-chip-cookie ice-cream sandwiches. I get a carton of vanilla ice cream and head toward the cash register. My heart jumps into my throat.

It's him.

Wyatt is standing at the register in a long black wool coat and black boots. I've seen him at The Horseman Inn a few times over the last week, but he was with his sister, so we didn't talk much. His eyes meet mine briefly and then drop to the snowstorm supply I'm carrying. "Just the essentials, huh?"

"I sense judgment." I try to see what he's buying, set out on the counter, but he shifts, his large shoulder blocking the view. He takes out his wallet and hands over a hundred-dollar bill to Nicholas. "Here. Keep the change." He grabs his items and tucks them inside his coat pockets. On the inside pockets too, like it's supersecret.

Nicholas looks concerned. "This is way too much, Wyatt. Hold on now. I'll get your change."

I grin and set my stuff on the counter. "Hmm…small enough for your pockets, but embarrassing enough to hide. What could it be?"

"None of your business," Wyatt mutters. Oh my God, the back of his neck is red. It must be something good. Wyatt turns to Nicholas. "Keep the change, really."

"I can still count just fine, young man!" Nicholas exclaims as he slowly digs through the cash drawer, getting a little huffy about a perceived age slight. He hands over the change, and Wyatt reluctantly takes it.

"Thanks," Wyatt grumbles.

"Is it a pack of cigarettes?" I ask, stepping close. "Nasty habit." I ruffle his hair to distract him as my other hand pulls open his unbuttoned coat. A box of tampons sticks out of his inside pocket.

His cheeks pinken. "Happy now? They're for my sister. Obviously."

My knees actually go weak, warmth stealing through me. None of my brothers would ever be caught dead buying me tampons. "Is that all?"

He looks to the ceiling, and the blush moves from his cheeks to the tips of his ears. "She had a craving for peanut M&M's."

I don't know what comes over me, but I suddenly want to spend time with this man. Like right away. "Maybe she'd like a chocolate-chip-cookie ice-cream sandwich too. I could make some for you both."

He studies me warily. It's almost like he thinks we don't normally get along. Ha-ha.

"I'm being sincere," I say. "It's nice what you do for her. My brothers would never—"

He cuts me off. "Sure, stop by with your ice-cream sandwiches. You guys can do the whole girl-talk thing."

"Okay. Lemme pay, and I'll be right over." I figure I can get in and out for a visit before the worst of the storm. It'll be hours before the roads are impassable. His place isn't far from mine.

He backs up a step, studying me for a moment before he nods once and leaves.

Nicholas scratches his head. "That one is a little odd, dontcha think?"

My mind goes back to the hippy founders of Summerdale, and the traditions we still have from them—shows performed in the big red barn, the found-items flotilla races, clam bakes at the lake, even though the clams are from the grocery store and don't grow in our lake. Our tamale-delivering mailman, among other odd people in town. "Actually, I think he fits right in."

~

The cookies are ready to go within an hour, and I know I should get going, but I find myself in my room, going through my clothes rack. The room is too small for a dresser, and the tiny closet holds my jackets and shoes. What I'm wearing—sweatshirt and jeans—won't do. I want to look presentable. I'm not trying to impress. Nothing like that. It's just important to take the time once in a while to look nice when you go out.

I settle on a soft green V-neck sweater with black skinny jeans and my high-heeled black leather ankle boots. Jenna calls them my first-date boots because they're impractical to wear for long, but they show off my legs. First dates are universally uncomfortable displays. Of course, *this* isn't a first date. I'm just visiting some friends, one who's in need of some womanly conversation, and one who isn't as bad as he seemed. I get that warm feeling in my chest again. I can hardly think someone who would buy his sister tampons is Satan. He definitely looked less satanic today, even with a red face.

I stop in my tiny bathroom for a quick visual inspection in the mirror. When I can finally afford an apartment of my own again, the first requirement will be counter space. This bathroom only has enough room for a pedestal sink, toilet, and small shower. It's all done in white, except the floor, which is black and white penny tiles. Very utilitarian. I pull my hair band out and grab a brush from the medicine cabinet, brushing out my long hair, one of my best features. I'm just being practical. When it's cold out, leaving my hair down keeps my neck warm. Just a little makeup to look presentable, a spritz of honeysuckle perfume, and I'm ready to go. My stomach flutters.

I put a hand to my stomach and take a calming breath. "This is not a date." I look myself in the eyes in the mirror. "Chill. Not a date."

I head out, grab my purse and the cookies, and stride to the stairway that leads to the rear exit of the restaurant. I'm halfway down the stairs when I realize I forgot the ice cream. I go back for it and leave again, mentally reviewing if I need anything else as I hurry down the steps. I'm not usually so scatterbrained.

I make the short drive to Wyatt's place, which I could theoretically walk to, except it's about a mile down a long road and then across a major thoroughfare with lots of drivers going more than the 50 mph speed limit, and at the top of a steep hill. Besides, it's freezing out, and I'm wearing my impractical boots. Not first-date boots. They're just *regular* boots that show off my long legs because I want to look presentable for friends. Really.

I park in his driveway and look over to my right at the lighthouse. Now that we're on speaking terms, would he give me a tour of it? It's just the kind of weirdness I love. I gather my bag of goodies and get out of the car, spotting Snowball in the window, barking at me.

"Hi, pretty girl!" I ring the doorbell and bounce on the balls of my feet, energy coursing through me.

The door pops open a few moments later to Wyatt holding Snowball like a football under his arm. "What's the password?" He looks left to right like there's spies around here.

I stifle a laugh. "Ice-cream sandwiches?"

"Close enough." He jerks his head and steps back to let me in.

I walk inside, looking around for any changes. Nothing different in the living room. I was here a little over a week ago, so I'm curious what the crew did.

He sets Snowball down. "I'm going upstairs for a minute. Go ahead to the kitchen." He gestures me toward it and heads upstairs.

Snowball looks up at me expectantly.

I walk toward the kitchen and Snowball follows. I set my stuff on the island counter and crouch to pet Snowball. "What a sweet pup you are," I coo. Her little tail wags and she goes up on her hind legs, putting her paws on my chest. "Aww, are you trying to hug me?" I stand and cuddle her close, stroking her silky fur. She leans her head against my neck.

Wyatt appears in the kitchen a few moments later, standing across the island from me, staring.

"What?" I ask.

"She really likes you. That's her hug when she puts her head on your neck and rests her paws on your shoulders."

I shift to look Snowball in the eye. "Of course you like me. I'm very likeable and I brought food." I set her on the ground, and she sits down, looking up at me adoringly.

Wyatt flashes a dazzling smile, and my breath quickens. When he's not smirking, he's stunning. There's something about that sexily rumpled dark hair, whiskey-colored eyes, and sensual lips. The beard is hot too. He's dressed casually in a navy thermal shirt, faded jeans, and sneakers.

I realize I've been checking him out a smidge too long. "I love your kitchen. Did you pick out this stuff or hire an interior designer?"

He spreads his arms. "All me, baby."

"I'm impressed."

He pulls his phone from his jeans' pocket. "I'll see what's keeping Kayla. I told her you were here." He presses a button and holds the phone up to his ear. A moment later, he asks her, "Are you coming down for ice-cream cookie sandwiches? They're freshly made." He shakes his head. "I told you not to eat all the M&M's. Sharing size means there's enough for two people." He listens for a moment. "I get the craving thing, but —no, I'm not mad. Okay, bye." He looks at me. "She stuffed herself with M&M's. Guess it's just us for ice-cream sandwiches."

"No problem. I'll make up a bunch and leave them in your freezer. She can have one whenever she's ready."

I get to work, unpacking the items. The cookies were still cooling when I left, so I figured I'd assemble them here. "I brought an ice-cream scoop. I didn't know if you'd have one."

"What am I, a caveman? We're fully stocked here with all the essentials. Ice-cream scoop, pizza slicer, marshmallow-roasting sticks."

"Except furniture."

He inclines his head. "I've got stuff in storage, and I'll buy more once the renovation is done. I'll get plates." He goes to a cabinet.

"Hi, Sydney." Kayla appears in the kitchen in an oversized gray sweatshirt, baggy sweatpants, and flip-flops. No makeup, her dark hair in a messy bun. "Thanks for bringing this stuff. Wyatt didn't tell me you were making ice-cream sandwiches until just now."

Wyatt sets a stack of large plates and napkins on the island. I shoot him a look. "You can't blame her for binging on chocolate if she didn't know."

"I thought she'd have better sen…" He trails off at Kayla's withering glare. "All good. You can have an ice-cream sandwich tomorrow."

I smile at her. "I'm going to make a bunch. You won't miss out."

"Thanks," she says. "I just haven't been feeling myself lately." She shuffles over to the sink, helping herself to a glass of water.

"Sorry to hear it." Wyatt mentioned she was heartbroken, and I don't know how serious it was, but it must've been a hard breakup if she went to big brother for help and stayed this long—it's been at least two weeks. My own breakups have been soothed just fine with the help of my friends. And even though it hurt, I always knew it was for the best. When something's not working, it's better to cut ties.

She opens the refrigerator. "Where's the wine?"

"You drank it," Wyatt says.

"Anything else alcoholic?" she asks.

"Whiskey," he replies. "The good stuff. Wasted on you, so don't even think about it."

She huffs and turns to me. "Do you have a bossy big brother?"

"I've got four brothers." I scoop vanilla ice cream onto a cookie. "Two older, two younger. Only the oldest bosses."

"It's the firstborn's privilege," Wyatt says with a smirk. I don't mind his smirk when it's directed at his sister.

"Any sisters?" Kayla asks, standing next to me at the island.

"Nope." I press a cookie on top of the ice cream for my first sandwich.

"Oh, that's sad," she says.

I turn to her, surprised. "Why do you say that?"

"Because sisters have a special bond."

I glance over at Wyatt, who took her in when she was heartbroken and bought her tampons. "I'd say your brother is doing a great job. I don't see any sisters around here taking such good care of you."

Her lower lip wobbles, and I shoot a look of alarm at Wyatt. His eyes soften as he looks at his sister.

"Sorry," I say. "Didn't mean to bring up a sore subject."

"It's fine," Kayla says. "They're just busy with their careers. One is in Chicago for the month for work, and the other is in the city for her big job, which has crazy hours, but she's also living with this guy, and there's no room for me. Wyatt's all I've got."

I suck in air, offended on his behalf. *All she's got?* He just shrugs.

I jab a finger at her. "You're *lucky* to have him. Now thank your brother for buying you tampons and chocolate. Geez, you think just any brother would do that? Mine wouldn't."

"It's fine," he says, holding up a palm. "She already thanked me."

Kayla's eyes go wide with shock. "They wouldn't? Not one of your brothers? Not even the oldest?"

"I don't think so." Not that I ever asked any of them to. I'm trying to imagine tough Drew braving the tampon aisle, or Adam with his reserved nature. Yeah, just don't see it.

"That's a shame," she says, her voice full of sympathy. "Sometimes when you need tampons the most, you feel the worst, and going out to the store is the very last thing you want to do."

"True," I say. "Guess I always thought I just had to suffer through the cramps alone. I get really irritable too. Like ragey."

"All right, can we get back to ice-cream sandwiches?" Wyatt asks. "Enough with the lady talk."

I hand him the first ice-cream sandwich.

"Thank you," he says, taking an aggressive bite. He chews for a moment. "Really good. The chocolate chips are melting in my mouth."

"Great contrast with the ice cream and perfect for a snowstorm," I say smugly. "And you questioned my snowstorm essentials." I get to work making more.

"Can I help you?" Kayla asks me.

"Sure. I'll scoop and you press the cookie on top."

We get into a rhythm making the sandwiches. Wyatt leaves, saying he has to take care of Snowball.

"So how long were you seeing the guy who broke your heart?" I ask.

She leans over the island, dropping her head in her hands. "Wyatt told you."

"Only because I saw you crying at my restaurant, so I wondered if you were okay. He just said you were heartbroken. No details. I'm a good listener if you want to talk about it." I squeeze her shoulder. "I promise to take your side and say evil things about your ex."

She straightens. "He is evil."

"Most exes are." I get back to work, scooping ice cream on a cookie and sliding it over to her to finish it.

She grabs a cookie and jams it on top. "He spent two months fawning over me, showering me with compliments and flowers and cards with mushy stuff inside. Super sweet stuff." Her voice cracks. "And then…"

When she doesn't fill in the sentence for several long moments, I make a guess. "He cheated on you."

"No! He proposed."

I scoop more ice cream, confused. "Oh. And you didn't want him to?"

She jams a cookie on top of my scoop of ice cream before I can even slide it over, and then breaks off a piece of cookie and pops it in her mouth. "Ooh, this is good. Did you just bake these?"

"Yup. Straight from the tube of premade dough." I put a

fresh cookie on top of the sandwich and shift the broken one onto a plate for her.

"So he proposed, I said yes, and we decided to have a secret elopement at our favorite Italian restaurant on New Year's Eve. It was going to be so romantic. He knew the owner, we got the town mayor to preside, and they closed the place so it would be private for our wedding." She sighs and breaks off another piece of cookie from the fresh one I just put there.

I shift the broken cookie and replace it with a new one, sliding it over. "Just press on that. Why was it a secret elopement?"

She stares at the fresh cookie. "Mostly to save money. We're both in grad school. I'm getting my master's; he's getting his PhD."

"Why not wait until you graduated?"

"He couldn't wait. That's what he said." She meets my eyes, her brows knit in confusion. "He wanted to marry me as soon as possible, and then he didn't show up." She grabs the fresh cookie and holds it up, shaking it. Bits of ice cream splatter on the counter. "I was left at the altar by that idiot!"

Not exactly an altar, but I get it. The guy backs out after being the instigator of a major romantic event. Makes no sense, but who can understand the male mind? They *think* they're being logical, but let's get real, their logic can get twisted with emotions just like women's. Of course, women more frequently draw the correct conclusion with the help of emotion. Guys get all turned around. They should make an emotion GPS to help get men back on track.

"Did he tell you why?" I ask.

"Cold feet!" she exclaims. "I mean, really. It was his idea to get married so quick. He sent a message through the restaurant owner, who was so sympathetic he offered to let me take our wedding food to go at no charge."

I shake my head. "That sucks big time. What's the plan for revenge?"

"Revenge?" she asks as if the idea never occurred to her.

"Yeah, you've got to do something for payback."

She stares at me. "Well, Wyatt wants to kick his ass, but I won't let him. I want my ex to think I'm over it."

"Were you in a wedding gown or just a nice dress?"

Her face crumples. "Wedding gown."

"Uh-huh. Payback. Maybe he left a favorite shirt at your place? Burn it. Do you know some of the same people? Let every woman know what he did. No one will ever want to date him. Except the crazy ones, who think they can change him. If you're really mad, and you think you can get to his car undetected, you could key the driver's side."

Her brows shoot up. "Have you ever done that stuff?"

"Mostly I burn my ex's stuff. It's cathartic. I may have made a voodoo doll and stabbed it in his junk multiple times." At her wide-eyed look, I add, "Kidding!" *I'm not crafty enough to make a voodoo doll. I imagined it in vivid detail.*

She pops a piece of cookie in her mouth and looks at me with admiration in her eyes. "Wow, Sydney, your mind veers toward evil. I hope you don't get involved with Wyatt because I'd hate to think what you'd do to him."

"I'd only want revenge if he broke my heart." Heat creeps up my neck. "I mean not that I'm—we're—you know." I can't exactly say we're friends. I don't know what we are.

She looks down at the melting ice cream on the cookie in front of her and puts her half-eaten cookie back on top. I give her one of the broken pieces from another cookie she ate part of to top it off. "Have you ever had your heart broken? I mean, just shattered?"

I wince. That must be how she feels. "Yeah, a few times. Twice after a year relationship. That seems to be the tipping point, a year. And then once in high school, but I don't know if that counts."

She squeezes my arm. "It all counts."

We finish up with the sandwiches, and I finally take one for myself. I realize Wyatt never came back.

"Where's your brother?" I ask.

"Probably hanging on the sofa with Snowball. That's where he usually is."

"Oh." My shoulders droop, and I immediately hitch them

up again. It seems he invited me over just to talk to his sister, not because he was interested in me.

That's cool. It's good to know these things up front before expectations can be raised and dashed.

In fact, it makes it that much easier to approach him for a business deal. I've been working up to it, trying to figure out terms we can both be happy with.

I'm *fine*.

8

Wyatt

Kayla and Sydney have been talking in the kitchen for a little over an hour. I hope it helped. I still don't know the name of the guy who rushed Kayla into a wedding and then dumped her. What kind of moron does that? I was sorely tempted to eavesdrop in case she dropped the name to Sydney, but I refrained. She needed the womanly bonding time. I do my best, but I remain sans ovaries.

It's around six, already dark outside, when Sydney pokes her head into the sofa room, where I'm camped out. "Hey, I'm going to head out before the snow gets bad."

I close my laptop and set it down on the far end of the sofa. Snowball takes the opportunity to climb into my lap, putting her front paws on my shoulders, and leaning her head against my neck. I put a hand on her back, accepting her hug. "How did she seem?"

Sydney closes the distance between us, and I lose focus, distracted by the way her green V-neck sweater clings to her sexy body. Long legs in black skinny jeans and high-heeled boots. She left her auburn hair down. I love that. Her hair's long, past her spectacular breasts, the kind of hair you can wrap around your fist like silken rope.

She speaks in a low tone. "Heartbroken, like you said, and so damn sweet she doesn't want revenge."

My gaze snaps to hers. "I want revenge for her."

"Me too. What an asshole."

I pat the sofa cushion next to me because we have a common goal now. I want to talk to her more. It's not because of that sexy sweater, though that doesn't hurt. Snowball thinks I patted the sofa for her, so she takes the seat. I shift her to my lap so Sydney can sit next to me.

She joins me, and I catch the scent of flowers. Sweet flowers, like summer in the middle of winter. I have to fight the urge to lean close and breathe her in.

She meets my eyes, oblivious to my growing lustiness. "I can't tell you everything she told me. Sisterhood code, you know."

Focus. This could be good intel. "Did she tell you the name of the guy?"

Her brows lift. Up close her eyes are a light brown with gold tones, reminding me of honey. Sydney with the honey eyes and sweet scent. It's natural to be drawn in. She's not sweet, which I like because sweet women always take offense to my direct way of speaking. Except Kayla, but she's used to me. Sydney looks and smells sweet, but with a fiery personality. *Want.*

"You don't know his name?" she asks.

I blink a few times, trying to remember what we were talking about. Oh, yeah, Kayla's ex. "I never met him. This whole thing was a nasty surprise."

She shakes her head. "She never actually said his name. Just that he was a PhD student."

"That narrows it down. How many could there be in the biostatistics program? She said they went to the same school." I shift Snowball to the floor, who gives me an aggrieved look, and retrieve my laptop. I click over to the university's website and search the biostatistics department for PhD students. Sometimes they'll list grad students if they work as teaching assistants.

Sydney looks over. "She didn't say he was in the same

program. They could've met in an overlapping class or at a student lounge or mixer or something."

I ignore her. I'm on the hunt. There's two PhD guys working as teaching assistants. Nerdy types like Kayla favors. I shut the lid. "I've got two potentials, but you're right, she could've went outside the program. She said they met online, and then she found out they went to the same school. Why can't she just spit out the name?"

Her eyes gleam. "What're you going to do to him?"

"I'd like to punch him in his stupid face." Snowball lifts her head from where she's curled at my feet.

Sydney nods eagerly. "Then what?"

I give her a wary look. Bloodthirsty, this one. "I hadn't gotten that far." Snowball curls up to sleep.

"You've got to kick him in the nuts," she says, as if this is obvious.

"Remind me never to get involved with you."

She stands and takes a step back. "Not a problem. You're not my type. At all. Actually, you're the opposite."

I ignore the jab, and the sinking feeling of disappointment. I kinda thought we were building something here. She talks to me a lot and came over to my place twice now. And I didn't miss the appraising look in her eyes when she first got here. She likes what she sees.

I keep my voice cool, instinctively knowing she'll run hot in response. "That's convenient because you're not my type either."

She crosses her arms, which gives her breasts a nice boost in that clingy sweater. "You probably exclusively date models."

I gesture wearily. "And actresses and heiresses. Anyone in the wealthy fundraiser circle." I sigh like it's a curse. Not that I mind beautiful women throwing themselves at me. I just wish it was actually me they were interested in, instead of my bank account. "That's who I meet. As a matter of fact—"

"I don't want to hear about your women," she snaps, those honey eyes flashing.

The blood rushes through my veins. "They're not mine.

They're on loan. Let me guess, your type is big dumb jocks."
My exact opposite.

"Why is that my type?"

"You know why."

"No, I don't."

"You care more about the package."

She jams her hands on her hips. "So now I'm shallow?" Her head swivels, and I know I'm in for it now. "Why the *hell* you think you know me well enough to predict my type is beyond me. You don't know me at all."

"Sure I do."

"No, you don't. Not even close."

This is so blatantly untrue I have to correct her. I tick everything off on my fingers. "You're broke, you have no business sense, you're hot tempered, which is great in bed and terrible in business, refer back to failing business, and you don't know when to cry uncle." At her silence, I think of one more so all five fingers are accounted for. "You're entirely too stubborn and independent, and it's not doing you any favors." Technically, six, but I keep to my one hand out.

She lifts her chin. "You prefer your women docile and dependent."

"I prefer a woman with good sense."

Her face flushes. "Go to hell!"

I might've played that wrong.

She flips me the bird and marches out of the room.

I really need to stop making her mad. It's not like I was trying to insult her. She *is* too stubborn and independent, struggling to keep that restaurant afloat, ignoring all my good suggestions, refusing to take a loan from Harper. I guess I get that with them being childhood friends, but still. The rest was all true, and she knows it.

I sit there for a few moments, debating if I should catch up to her and apologize. She did come out here in a snowstorm to cheer up my sister and brought homemade ice-cream cookie sandwiches.

I head back through the kitchen and find Kayla sitting on

top of the island, scrolling on her phone. Snowball follows me in.

Kayla looks up. "Sydney just left in a hurry."

I ignore the stab of guilt. "She was trying to get home before the storm got bad."

Snowball looks up at me expectantly. Her people barometer approved of Sydney.

I screwed up.

Sydney

Damn him! Softening me up with that protective big-brother stuff, and then wham! Insult city. To think I came out here in the middle of a snowstorm with ice-cream sandwiches to help out his sister! This is how he thanks me. By insulting me, my restaurant, and my good sense!

No more. I am done with Wart forever.

Even the pelting snow can't touch the heat of my anger. I step outside just as the storm is picking up, the trees bending with the wind. I make my way over to my old black Honda, yank open the trunk, and grab the ice scraper. Front windshield. Back. Side windows. I toss the scraper back in the trunk and dash back to the driver's side, getting inside. Crap. I left my ice-cream scoop in his kitchen. I should've taken that and all my ice-cream sandwiches with me. He doesn't deserve any of my snowstorm essentials. Now I have to go home with nothing.

I shiver and consider going back inside for my stuff. I don't want him to enjoy my food. I want him to eat dirt. *Forget it.* I just want to get out of here. I start the car and blast the heat. I swear he's insulted me for the last time, and if I never have to see him again, I will be one happy camper.

I slowly ease forward, not wanting my tires to spin on the fresh snow. A monstrous crack rends the air right before a huge pine tree looms overhead. I scream as it crashes right in front of my car. The car shakes from the near miss. The tree trunk on its side is nearly as high as my car. I put a hand over my pounding heart, adrenaline rushing through my veins.

I could've been killed.

Oh my God.

I could've been *killed*.

My hands are shaking. I blink a few times, still in shock. *Okay, it's okay.* I'm alive. That's the important part.

My brain starts to function again. I can't drive around this tree. It's too massive, cutting across his front lawn. It just missed the lighthouse too. If I can't drive around it, that could only mean…oh no. No, no, no. I can't be stuck here.

He is the very last person I want to see right now or ever again.

I pull out my phone and call Drew. He has a pickup truck that's good in the snow. As soon as he answers, I blurt out, "A pine tree came down in front of my car, and I can't get around it. Can you pick me up?"

"Where are you?"

I wince. He's going to want to know what the hell I'm doing at Satan's house. Last he heard, that's what I called him. Probably should've stuck with my instincts there. "Still in town. At a friend's house across Route 15."

"Route 15 is a mess. Trees and heavy branches all over it. Eli's out there with the highway department right now. It's not safe. And I don't want you walking home either. Just stay put. Which friend?"

He knows Jenna and Audrey live close to the center of town. I hate to admit the truth. I feel so foolish risking going out in a storm just because I was mistakenly attracted to the wrong man.

"Syd, what friend?"

"Wyatt," I admit.

"Are you going to be okay there? I could talk to him, give him a warning."

I fidget, embarrassed at the thought of my big brother intervening on my behalf. I can handle Wyatt. I don't want to handle Wyatt, but I can. "No, it's fine. His sister is here. I'll just hang with her."

"What were you doing out in this mess anyway?"

Following a man with tampons.

I sigh. "I was visiting his sister. She's going through a hard time."

"Check in with me or Eli tomorrow. One of us will get you as soon as the roads are cleared."

"Okay, thanks."

I hang up and stare at the pine tree that did me the favor of not killing me, and then forced me to spend more time with the last person on earth I want to see. It'll be a while before a tree guy can get out here to remove the tree. I take a few deep breaths, attempting to calm down so I can face Satan like a rational person.

I can't believe I have to spend the night with my mortal enemy! Damn you, tree!

I startle at a knock on the window.

Wyatt stares at me. "Are you okay?"

9

———

Wyatt

That horrific noise I heard was a giant pine tree crashing across my driveway. It landed inches from Sydney's car. She could've been killed.

She's not responding, just sitting there, staring at the tree in shock. No blood. Thank God. Snow pelts me, thrown by the roaring wind, the trees creaking in the gusts. The snow must be weighing down the trees, making it easier for them to break or topple.

I knock on the window again. "Sydney?"

She keeps staring at the tree in front of her car. Maybe she got whiplash from slamming on the brakes.

I open the door. "Sydney, are you okay?"

She slowly turns to me. "Yeah, I'm okay."

I offer my hand and help her out of the car, stopping to go back for her purse and shutting the door. She shivers, crossing her arms against the cold. "I can't get around this tree. Drew says the roads aren't passable either."

"Okay. Come back inside before any more trees come down." I drop my arm around her shoulders and guide her into the house.

I shut the front door behind us just as a huge tree branch

crashes nearby. She grabs me, hugging me tight around the middle. *Pure instinct. Nothing personal.* She must be terrified.

I drop her purse and wrap my arms around her, holding her head to my chest. She feels right in my arms. No one has ever felt so right. *Okay, think. What does she need?* No question she's spending the night. It's not safe out there. I loosen my hold on her, suddenly realizing the strength it'll take to keep my distance. I'm not taking advantage of the situation. She's upset and probably not happy she's stuck here. *Is it bad that I'm glad she's here a little longer?* I get a second chance to connect with her, even if the circumstances aren't ideal. I like her.

She pulls away. "Sorry."

"No problem. I'm sorry about before. I shouldn't have said that stuff about your restaurant and your sense." Though one could argue it wasn't very sensible to visit us during a major snowstorm, but I'm glad she did, so I keep my mouth shut. And her business *is* failing, but now is not the time for inconvenient truths. I'm mending fences for a long night ahead. I don't want a war.

"Okay," she says quietly.

Snowball wanders over. She must've been too scared of the tree crash to bark. I scoop her up. "You want to hold her?" *A fluffy buffer. Perfect.*

"Sure." She takes Snowball and cuddles her close. Snowball wriggles happily, her tail wagging. Sydney is Snowball approved, and I should take that seriously. She's growled at most of my girlfriends. Not that Sydney's my girlfriend, but there is definitely chemistry, even if it sometimes blows up.

I gesture for Sydney to follow me into the sofa room. She follows at a slow pace. Kitchen's empty. Kayla must've read the situation and figured I had it taken care of. She probably watched through the window and, knowing Kayla, she was giving us some time alone together. She's been saying it's time I stop wasting my time on women who don't deserve me. She worships her big brother. Rightly so.

"We can watch something on my laptop if you want," I say once we reach the sofa room. "You can sleep on the sofa later." I don't bother to look back for her reaction, which I'm sure is horrified. She left in a hurry because I pissed her off, and now she's spending the night with me. Not *with me*. Adjacent to me.

The normally fiery Sydney remains silent. She's starting to worry me.

I gesture for her to take a seat. "I'll get a fire started."

She points at the sofa. "I can't take your bed. Where will you sleep?"

I'm so relieved she sounds normal again I nearly smile. I shrug one shoulder like I couldn't care less. I should've bought a sleeper sofa, but how was I to know Kayla would show up and need my bed? And I know she's my sister, but it feels weird to even think about sharing a bed with her. "I'll figure something out."

"Like what?"

I crouch in front of the fireplace and toss some kindling on the log. "I can sleep on the floor with a throw pillow and use my winter coat as a blanket." Feeling downright Dickensian in here. *That's me, a billionaire Oliver Twist.*

The obvious solution, which I'm not going to mention, is putting petite Kayla on the sofa, while Sydney and I take the queen-size bed upstairs. But that's not going to happen. She's upset by her close call. And it was only a few short weeks ago that Sydney seethed at the mere sight of me. Just because I gave her some constructive criticism on her failing restaurant.

I glance back at her over my shoulder.

She sits on the sofa gingerly. "Well, uh, thanks for having me."

"Of course." I add more kindling and light the long match. I love having a fireplace. I could never do this at my apartment in the city. "At least we have ice-cream sandwiches."

I light the kindling and shake the match out. I look at her over my shoulder. "Believe it or not, I've got real food too."

"Yeah, like what?"

I turn back to the fire and retrieve the iron poker to shift the kindling a bit. Looks like the fire's burning on the log now. I put the tool back and stand. "I've got leftover Chinese and the makings for two kinds of sandwiches, turkey or PB&J."

She flashes a smile, and my gut tightens. She's stunningly beautiful when she smiles. "What else do you need?"

I point a finger at her. "Ice-cream cookie sandwiches."

"We're all set, then. Thanks again for having me. I know it's an inconvenience."

"Corpse in the driveway is an inconvenience. Your company is a pleasure."

Her jaw drops and then clamps shut.

"I'm glad you're okay," I add.

"Me too," she says quietly.

A beat passes in silence, the only sound the crackling of the fire and the wind ripping through the trees. My pulse thrums through my veins, the moment suddenly feeling charged.

Snowball jumps down from Sydney's lap and trots over to me.

Sydney gets up and goes to the side window, peering behind the temporary shade I put up. "The snow's really piling up."

I look around for my laptop and realize Kayla must've taken it upstairs with her. "You want me to get my laptop? We could watch something."

"That's okay."

So I guess we're talking. Probably best to do that from a distance. Snowball is curled in front of the fire now. I go to retrieve her bed from the side of the sofa just as Sydney settles into the corner of the sofa. She peers over the arm of it, watching me.

"You got your dog a pink monogrammed bed?" she asks.

I can hear the laughter in her voice. "She came with it. Besides, how would she know which bed was hers if her name wasn't on it?"

She laughs, a throaty sound that grabs me by the balls. I might like that as much as her flashing eyes and fiery temper.

I cross the room, scoop up Snowball, and place her in her bed by the hearth. She sighs. Not too close for sparks to reach her, but close enough for the heat. Then I take the large plastic cup with her grooming stuff from the mantel and sit cross-legged on the floor next to her.

"First things first," I tell Snowball. "You know the drill." I pull her into my lap, and she gives me an annoyed look. I add a dab of poultry-flavored toothpaste to her toothbrush and get to work.

"You brush your dog's teeth?" Sydney asks.

I stay focused, making sure I get her fangs up to the gum line. "She can't do it herself, can she?"

"I guess not. I just didn't know that was a thing."

"It's especially important for shih tzus because of their underbite. It's easy for her teeth to rot, and then the vet has to pull 'em." Her previous owner told me everything I needed to know.

Sydney gets quiet. I sense she's watching our nightly routine. I need to get it out of the way before I get distracted by Sydney and forget. Besides, it'll give her time to get comfortable being here with me. I think this is the longest we've talked without a glare from her end. I never glare. I smirk. Mostly when something entertains me. Sydney goes crazy for my smirks.

After I finish with Snowball's teeth, I get out the soft wipe to clean her eyes and ears. She tolerates it well. It's a ritual she's had since she was a puppy. "Looking good," I tell Snowball once I'm finished. "Now you can snooze by the fire." I set her back in her bed, and she curls up, looking content.

I put away the grooming stuff and turn to Sydney, who's looking at her phone. "I'll wash my hands and get started with dinner. Still just the one bathroom. It's upstairs if you need it."

"Thanks," she says softly.

I'm tempted to follow up on that softness, the first I've ever heard from her, but I need to wash up first.

After washing my hands in the bathroom upstairs, I check myself out in the mirror and smooth my hair back. I need a haircut. My hair can get unruly with the thick waves. If I ever grew it long, I'm sure it would look just like Kayla's. Speaking of…

I knock on her door and then open it when she doesn't respond. She's sitting up in bed with my laptop on her lap and earbuds in.

She takes one earbud out. "How's it going with Sydney? Is she recovering from her near miss?"

"Yeah, and she's spending the night. Can't move the tree or go out in this storm. Come downstairs with us and bring the laptop." I need someone between us so I'm not tempted to make a move. Sydney is vulnerable and shaken, forced to be here. I can't take advantage.

A smile plays over her lips, her brown eyes sparkling. "Oh, I don't know. Maybe you'd like to get to know each other a little better." She gives me a big exaggerated wink.

A lick of panic goes through me. "She'd be more comfortable if you were there. Besides, you have the laptop."

"God forbid you actually talk to a woman and get to know her."

"I know her plenty. And you want dinner, right? So, come down. You can talk to Sydney while I get it ready."

She waves in the air. "I can grab a sandwich whenever, or some of that leftover lo mein." She cocks her head. "So what are the sleeping arrangements?"

"She gets the sofa, and I'll take the floor. Would you please just come down for a while?"

"But you don't have any extra blankets. How will you stay warm?"

Clearly, she's not joining us.

I give up. "I'll use my winter coat."

Her brow furrows in concentration before she brightens. "I know. I'll ask her if she'd like to have a slumber party with me. We can share the bed, and you can have the sofa."

"Fine." I turn to go.

"Are you mad because you wanted to have her all to yourself?"

I turn back. "I'm not mad. I asked you to join us." *I didn't want temptation within reach, and now it won't be. It's a slumber party night for the women. I'll be alone with my furry companion like usual. Fine.*

I head for the door.

"Not everyone is like Julia," Kayla says softly.

I stiffen and then shake my head and walk out the door. My sisters believe Julia screwed with my head and that's the reason I haven't had a serious relationship in three years. That's *not* why. Did she betray me? Yes. But I'm over it. In fact, after two years with her, I realized my biggest mistake was settling down too soon. You should enjoy your twenties and meet lots of different people. Have fun, all that shit.

Now that I'm thirty, same deal. Why the hell not?

10

———

Wyatt returns with an irritated expression on his face.

It must be because of me. He's annoyed he has to put up with an unexpected overnight guest booting him from his own bed. "I won't be a bother to you."

He jolts like I surprised him. He must've been deep in thought. "What?"

"I don't want to be an inconvenience. I'll just make myself a sandwich and play games on my phone. You won't even notice I'm here. And I'll sleep on the floor with my winter coat, okay? You can still use your usual stuff and sleep on the sofa."

He stares at me. "What the hell are you talking about?"

"Me not being a bother?"

"You're not. And I'm not making you sleep on the floor either. Ridiculous. Come on. We'll get dinner."

He still seems pissed off about something. Maybe Kayla got on his nerves. I know siblings can get under your skin super quick.

I follow him into the kitchen. "Your sister seems cool."

"Yeah." He taps the island with both hands. "So what would you like for dinner?"

"Whatever you don't want."

He shakes his head, muttering to himself as he walks over to the refrigerator. He takes out four containers of Chinese food and sets them on the island, rattling off the contents. "Pick."

"Can I have a little of everything?"

"Yup."

He takes out plates and utensils. Then he gestures for me to serve myself first. He's being monosyllabic in that guy way, when they're trying not to share what's bothering them. We don't know each other well enough for me to push, so I let him stew, figuring it'll pass soon. That's how it is with my brothers and the three guys I got serious enough about to get to know their moods.

I help myself, careful to leave enough for him and Kayla.

He sticks my plate in the microwave without a word and helps himself, piling food on his plate. After our dinners are warmed up, we eat sitting at the kitchen island in silence. It's a cozy silence, actually, the room warm and bright compared to the raging storm outside. I can hear the roar of the wind through the trees in the distance.

"I hope we don't lose power," I say.

His forkful of broccoli halts halfway to his mouth. "That would suck. Does it happen a lot around here?"

"Do you consider three or four times a year a lot?"

"Yes."

"Then yeah."

"Why didn't the Realtor tell me about that? I would've taken precautions."

I twirl some lo mein around my fork. "They were probably so happy they finally sold this place, they didn't want to mention anything bad. It's the wind that's the problem, taking out tree branches and whole trees—as you've seen— that knock down power lines. And it takes a while for the power company to get to us here. Even before the power company can go to work, our highway department has to clear out the downed trees, and then the power company can deal with the wires. We have a generator at The Horseman Inn for the basics. You should get one here." I chew lo mein.

I'm surprisingly hungry considering I had an ice-cream sandwich not long ago. Guess nearly dying sparked an appetite. I'm just so grateful to be sitting here, warm, fed, safe from the storm. Who knew I could feel so good trapped with Wyatt Winters?

He makes a face. "We're really in the sticks out here. First I find out I'm on well water and septic, and now I have to make my own electricity. What's next? We have to cook our food over an open fire?"

"Be prepared for anything. Obviously you were never a Boy Scout."

One corner of his mouth lifts in a small smile that has me smiling back. His earlier mood is passing, replaced by the Wyatt I know and love. *Like. I like. Sometimes.* "I was too busy taking apart computers and building something better."

"Ah, you were one of those indoor cats holed up in your basement cave, working on computers." I cough out, "Nerd."

He points his fork at me. "I'll have you know as the first-born and only boy, I had my own room to hole up in. Anyway, it paid off. Sold my first tech startup at nineteen and two more since." He digs into his dinner with gusto.

I take a few more bites, considering what he does with his time. "I heard you were retired, but you must dabble with tech in your spare time just for the hell of it, right? What're you working on now?"

"No way. I don't want to be chained to a computer anymore. I've seen the light." He squints and looks to the ceiling. "And it's the sun."

I laugh. "Okay, so you discovered you can go outdoors, so now what?"

"I'm renovating this house."

"And?"

"And then I chill."

I take a drink of water. "That's boring."

He gazes into my eyes, his voice husky. "Not so far."

I look away, my cheeks flushing. That was…hot. And it was barely a flirt. I just felt the intention low in my belly, where I now ache. Nope. I'm not lusting for the man I planned to ask for a loan. Now that we're on civil terms, I should bring that up and then lay out how I would pay him back with interest. I don't want him to think I'm after his money. Well, I am, but it would be for a mutually beneficial transaction. If I could only figure out what I have to offer in return besides a piece of my restaurant. That's a hard line I won't cross.

And it goes without saying we'd keep everything strictly professional. Sex and business don't mix. Not that Wyatt and I are about to have sex. God, it's been so long I'm becoming obsessed. I need to sign up for one of those dating apps to meet someone.

Fact is, if I cross the line with him, he won't respect me as a businesswoman. And that respect is *everything*. I want to be taken seriously. I know my stuff. I just stepped into a difficult situation.

I sense his stare. He's not eating, just studying me. We're close enough I catch his clean scent and the faint smell of woodsmoke. My gaze drops to his lips, those sensual lips. I lick my own lips. I suddenly notice the shimmering silence, ripe with possibility, and meet his smoldering eyes just like in my dreams. My breath hitches, a shiver of excitement racing down my spine. *Say something!* "So what happens after you finish the renovation?" My voice sounds high. I clear my throat. "Are you going to buy another old place to renovate?"

He goes back to his dinner, scooping up some chicken. "I don't know. Haven't thought that far ahead."

I finish my meal, my thoughts bouncing all over the place. What's next? Intimate conversation by the fire? Watching a movie together on his laptop? Throwing my arms around him again? It felt so good to be held in his arms. Like nothing could touch me in that safe haven. And this from the man I thought was put on earth to harass me!

Chill, Syd. Ask him for the loan. Keep it professional.

He clears our dishes and turns back to me. "C'mon, back to the only seat in the house."

I follow him back to the sofa and look to the crackling fire, Snowball curled up in her little bed in front of the fireplace.

"She must love it by the fire because she didn't even look for scraps in the kitchen when we ate."

"She always sleeps after her night routine. Her dinner was at three, and she doesn't expect more until morning."

I eye the sofa. There's three cushions. I take the end cushion to keep a professional distance. He takes the other end cushion and gives me a tight-lipped smile, looking uncomfortable. It makes me feel like even more of an inconvenience. Crap. How can I ask him for a loan when he looks so uncomfortable?

I fall back on small talk. "Have you been up in the lighthouse?"

He chuckles and wiggles his fingers at me. "You mean my secret lair?"

I shift toward him eagerly. "What's it like?"

His lips twitch. "Swear you won't tell anyone?"

"Ooh, there's something good hiding in there." I hold up a palm. "I swear!"

He leans in, saying in a conspiratorial voice, "It's not a lighthouse."

"It's not? Damn, that's so disappointing. Of course, it never made sense to have one up here on dry land."

"It's a water tower, and the last owner made it up to look like a lighthouse because he liked lighthouses."

A water tower makes a lot more sense on a former farm. "Mystery solved." I crinkle my nose. "I think I'll let it be a mystery for the rest of town. It's more fun that way."

"Course you will. You swore a blood oath."

I lift my brows. "Not quite but your secret's safe with me. I wonder why nobody knows about it."

He leans back, stretching his arms across the back of the sofa. "You'd have to come up on the property and investigate it up close. I don't think the former owner had many visitors. He was a widower, and his son died young. I looked into the history."

"That's sad. He must've been lonely."

"Most likely. Hopefully he had a dog."

I smile. "I never pictured you as the kind of guy with a little white dog named Snowball."

"Are you saying her name doesn't fit? She looks like a snowball." Snowball lifts her head, gazes tiredly at Wyatt, and goes back to sleep.

"No, *you* don't fit."

"Yeah? What kind of dog should I have?"

I immediately picture a smug-looking dog I saw on a meme once with no regrets for licking his owner's sandwich. "A Great Dane."

"Because?"

"Uh, no reason."

He leans close, smiling, looking more charmer than smug. My pulse speeds like crazy. "Come on, I can take it."

"Because you, uh, sometimes look smug like this Great Dane meme who licked peanut butter off his owner's sandwich when he wasn't looking. Before, I mean, when I saw you at my restaurant. Now you're okay." *Good save. Ask him about the loan.*

He presses his lips together, his eyes dancing with amusement. "I'm not smug. I'm just right."

My temper flares. "Criticizing doesn't make you right." *It makes you smug in your so-called superior knowledge.*

"Sydney, Sydney, Sydney, I'm not criticizing. I'm giving helpful suggestions for your restaurant. It could be improved in many ways. I know it, and I'm letting you know it. You're welcome."

I narrow my eyes.

He points at me. "I've been waiting for the squinty-eyed glare. The natural state of your face around me."

My shoulders tense. I tell myself to calm down. He took me in and fed me. He's giving me his bed. Not that I'm going to take it. The point is, I don't want to fight with him. I want to work out a business deal. How can one man be both generous and aggravating at the same time?

He smirks, and I swear he knows how much that smirk irritates me. He wants to fight. I refuse. I'm here as a guest in his home, and I will be gracious and kind. I unclench my fists.

"So," I say brightly, "what should we do now?" It's my subtle way of saying we should stop talking because it's only going to lead to a blowout, and then where would I go? I'm stuck here with the man who seems to be one part devil, one part angel.

"I'd offer you a drink, but I'm out of wine thanks to the lush upstairs, and I doubt you like whiskey."

"Why do you say that?"

"Women tend to go for the sweet fruity drinks. Not that you're sweet, though your eyes do remind me of honey."

I fight back a smile, warmth stealing through me. That was kind of a compliment right there. His eyes remind me of whiskey, but I keep that to myself. "Most guys think I'm edgy enough to handle a hard drink." What can I say? I make no apologies for being a strong woman who speaks her mind.

He gestures around my head. "Edgy would be spiked hair and piercings. You must go to the salon regularly like my sister Paige. Masses of auburn hair with a slight wave."

I guess having sisters he knows hair shades. I'm beyond flattered by his description. "I go to the salon once a year for a trim. This is natural."

He reaches out like he wants to touch it and then drops his hand. "Wow. Paige would kill for your hair. Hers takes a team for highlights and styling, and I don't even know what else."

I blush, my lashes fluttering down. "Thank you."

"Plus your clothes always cling to your curves like you're letting the world know you're a sexy woman. Edgy has something to prove. You're just confident."

My jaw gapes at the outrageous compliment even as heat flashes through me. *He thinks I'm sexy.*

He continues as if he hasn't just said the most flirty, flattering thing. "Just an incontrovertible fact. Ask anyone."

It's as if he's constructed a logical argument for why I'm not edgy. He sees me as a confident, beautiful sexy woman. I have never been so complimented in my life. And even though whiskey is great on a cold winter night, I don't ask for a drop. My defenses are crashing down around me as it is. I don't need my inhibitions to fly out the window too.

"Thank you, Wyatt."

He tilts his head, his eyes softening. "Fact."

I desperately want to close the distance, to feel his arms around me again. The cushion between us feels like a huge space to cross. I can't seem to move. If he wanted me close, he's the kind who'd just say it. Look at how plainly he laid out the "fact" that I'm a sexy woman with great hair.

Wait, what am I thinking? I'm not crossing the line with my future business associate. I'm suddenly afraid he can see all the different impulses racing through me—wanting to get closer, needing to keep some boundaries.

I focus on the fire, anything but my intense attraction to him. Those compliments just made me feel all gooey. "I understand why Kayla drank all the wine. It's an integral part of the breakup process, along with ice cream or chocolate. For me, I'll eat a pint of chocolate ice cream—"

"Chocolate, the natural antidepressant for women."

"Uh-huh, and then I burn any pictures or souvenirs of the relationship in effigy."

He leans forward. "You do that a lot?"

"Not a lot."

"Truth time. How many serious boyfriends have you burned in effigy?"

"Three serious exes. One for catharsis more than anything. He was my high school boyfriend. We went to separate colleges and that was that."

"Why did you break up with the other guys?"

"One because we just kept fighting and it obviously wasn't working, and one because…"

He looks at me expectantly.

I swallow hard. "Just because."

He looks over to the fire. "Don't tell me."

"He said he wasn't in love with me anymore." I cross my arms at my middle, hugging myself. That one was rough.

He turns back to me, his voice surprisingly gentle. "Were you still in love with him?"

"Well, yeah. It was a shock to hear."

He shakes his head. "He was probably cheating on you."

"What?"

"I'm just saying how could anyone be in love and then suddenly not be in love? There was probably someone else."

I frown. "That's even worse. I never asked questions. I just moved on."

"My ex slept with my former best friend. They're married now."

My eyes widen. He said it so matter-of-factly, but I know that must've hurt. "Oh shit. How did you find out?"

"I came home one day, and they were both there, sitting at the dining room table, looking serious. They said they had something to tell me."

"No! They ambushed you on your own turf! What did they say?"

"She said she wasn't in love with me anymore. See, not just you that bullshit happens to. And then they shared that they're in love with each other, it's serious, and they plan on getting married."

"What did you do when they dropped that bomb on you? I'd be seeing red."

"I go cold when I'm furious, so I said, thanks for telling me, now get out, and I don't ever want to see either of you again. Then I got the hell out. Sold my house—this was in California—and moved to Manhattan. I didn't want any reminders of either of them."

"How long ago was that?"

"Three years."

He probably hasn't had a real relationship since. It would be hard to trust again with a double betrayal. "Wow, that's way worse than my breakup story."

He grins crookedly. "I win."

It's a sad grin, and I just want to hug him. A well of emotion rises in my chest for all he's shared. He's surprisingly open and honest. It makes me want to talk even more, to find out everything there is to know about him. I actually really like him. And not in that professional way I'm trying to hang onto. This is not good. I know it, but I can't help but be sucked in. How many guys would let themselves be vulnerable like that?

He changes the subject. "Have you lived in Summerdale your whole life?"

"Most of it. I moved away for college and lived in Hoboken for a while for work before I came home to take over the restaurant. How about you? Did you grow up in California?"

"New Jersey. My mom is a history professor at Princeton University. My dad was a math professor there before he died."

"How old were you when you lost him?"

"Thirteen." He pounds his chest with both hands. "Man of the family right here."

My heart squeezes painfully. I know that feeling. I took over a lot of the cooking and cleaning my mom used to do, and fussed over my youngest brother. I was the woman of the family. "My mom died when I was twelve, so I get it. I was the only girl, and her responsibilities fell to me. I mean, I wanted to help, to try to make it feel like she was still with us. She was a nurse and my dad..." My voice chokes. "God, it's been a year now, and it still feels fresh." I blink back tears. I hate crying. "The Horseman Inn was his business. I'm fourth generation. It went to Drew, the oldest brother. He said it was a money pit, and then I stepped in to save it."

He's quiet, his eyes soft.

I take a calming breath.

"It's tough to lose a parent," he finally says. "My dad died from a heart attack—bam, out of the blue, gone—just as teen hormones hit me." He looks to the ceiling. "Great timing, Dad." He turns back to me. "But I rose to the occasion, took care of my sisters, and helped out my mom when she needed it."

Now I understand why Kayla ran to him during her crisis, and why she thought it was normal for him to take care of her feminine hygiene needs. He's *always* taken care of her. She looks young. She must've been little when their dad died.

"I was lucky I had two older brothers, and my dad

stepped up, becoming more hands-on as a parent. They took care of me while I took care of the house and my younger brothers."

"Three guys raised you through your teen years?" He tugs a lock of my hair. "No wonder you're such a tough cookie."

I smile widely. "Not tough, strong."

"All right, Sydney, you've earned it. I'll share my whiskey with you." He stands and offers his hand. "It's the good stuff meant to savor."

I stare at that offered hand, the invitation to get closer, and hesitate. My brain screams to keep my distance. But the rest of me? It's an impossible pull to resist.

I place my hand in his, warmth enveloping my smaller hand as he helps me up. "I'll be sure to report back on the full-bodied palate and finish."

"Mmm, I like when you talk whiskey to me."

Our gazes lock for a charged moment before he gives my hand a tug, guiding me to the kitchen.

11

———

Over a small glass of expensive whiskey, we laugh our asses off about our younger siblings' shenanigans. I had to share when six-year-old Caleb mooned the audience at his school play because he thought it was funnier than the boring play, and I have sworn on my life not to repeat some of what his sisters have done. *Hee-hee, but I know what I know, Kayla, Paige, and Brooke!*

Now we're both pretty mellow and smiling a lot.

Wyatt leans across the kitchen island toward me. "You want me to wrench the laptop out of Kayla's grip so we can watch a movie or something?"

I laugh. "She can join us."

He straightens. "Which I told her. She's probably wrapped up in one of her shows. She's been binge-watching a lot, ever since she was left at the altar, so to speak. Technically, she was left at a table."

I smother a giggle. He wags his finger at me, smiling.

He gestures magnanimously. "Or we could talk some more."

"About what?"

"I don't know. Isn't that what women like to do, talk?"

I pretend slap him, waving a hand in front of his face. "For someone with three sisters, you're kinda sexist."

"I'm not sexist. I *understand* women because I have three sisters. They love to talk."

"Not all woman are like your sisters."

He presses his hands together like he's praying and looks to the ceiling. "Thank God for that."

I laugh. "You're lucky Kayla didn't hear you say that."

He grins. "I know. So…looks like it's back to the sofa for more talk, talk, talk." He lets out a big sigh, even as his eyes sparkle with good humor. He joins me at my side and then gestures for me to go ahead.

I take a seat on the end cushion, where I sat before, and he takes the center cushion right next to me. I'm glad. He smells good, woodsy, and I feel close to him after talking so much. The whiskey makes me feel nice and mellow. Or maybe that's just having him near.

"So what's new with Sydney Robinson?"

I love hearing him say my whole name in his deep baritone. Correctly too. No Cindy business. "Nothing new. I've spent the last six months trying to bring The Horseman Inn to a thriving place of business that would make my father proud."

A hint of a smirk crosses his face. "Yet you won't take any of my helpful suggestions."

Even whiskey mellow, that smirk irritates me. "Our beer is fine."

"Your beer sucks. Plus you need to upgrade the menu."

I hold up my palm. "I don't want to fight with you."

"So don't."

I shift to face him. "You're starting to piss me off."

"Why? It's an incontrovertible fact. The place needs improvement, so improve it."

"It's not that easy! We're near bankruptcy. My dad—never mind."

"Your dad left you in debt, right? No way you could've run it into the ground in only six months, especially never spending money on improvements. You're trying to protect his memory just like he protected you by hiding his financial troubles."

My lips part in surprise. "How did you know he hid them?"

He shrugs. "It's what an overprotective father would do. Because he loved you and didn't want you to worry. My dad did the same to us. He invested in the stock market and ultimately lost a lot of money. Funny, as analytical as he was, he bought and sold mostly on emotional impulse. Buying stuff on the rise and selling in a panic when it was cratering. I saw the financial statements. My mom managed to slowly get out of debt. Fortunately, my sisters and I went to college tuition-free at Princeton since my mom was a professor. It all worked out. How much debt are you in?"

"Two hundred thousand. I'm making monthly payments, but if I miss a payment, they're starting the foreclosure proceedings. I missed three payments already last quarter. Every month I'm scraping the money together. I've got January's payment thanks to the New Year's Eve fundraiser. February, I don't know." I let out a breath. "It's really stressful going month to month, not knowing how much longer I can keep it alive."

He takes all that in stride. "Sure. Plus you need more money for improvements."

"Yes, if I go that route."

"You have to go that route to survive." He lifts a palm. "I could help you out. I could invest in your business, but we'd have to be equal partners. I'd want a say in it."

I was expecting it, but still, everything in me recoils. This is my family's legacy, no outsiders. *Negotiation time.*

"One more thing," he says. "You can't get all pissy and lose your temper while we're working together. That's not going to work for me and, honestly, it's the main reason I haven't offered before. Sure, it's entertaining when nothing's on the line—"

"Entertaining?" I echo incredulously. "I was legit mad."

"But I don't want to battle every time we need to make a change. Obviously, big changes will need to be made to save the place. Status quo is not working."

I bristle. Like it's *my* fault we fought before. He purposely antagonizes me. I loosen my clenched jaw. I must rise above and show him just how professional I can be.

"That's a nice offer, Wyatt, but I don't want a partner. I was hoping for a loan I'd pay back with interest." *Over a long period of time.*

"Go to a bank, then."

I stiffen. *Didn't Harper already tell him my situation?* He's trying to box me in with logic and force his way into my restaurant. "I did try banks."

"No go, huh? Not surprised. Banks don't want to loan money to someone deep in debt. They're skittish that way."

I stare straight ahead, trying to figure out any leverage I might have. I hate that he has all the power here. His money. But it's my place. Every other Robinson did just fine on their own. Well, except Dad, but I'm sure that wasn't his fault. The town was in a transition stage, where more people were moving away to retire and not many moving in. It's only recently that young families have taken notice of Summerdale. Probably because our high school was ranked as one of the best in the state.

"Here's the truth," he says, "you've been running the place for six months, and it's failing. Bring me on, and it'll succeed. I've launched three successful businesses on my own. The last one I sold to a social media giant for a ridiculous amount. Not to mention the half dozen struggling businesses I acted as consultant and investor for and made profitable. I get the job done, and everyone is better off for it."

"So modest," I grumble.

"Just the facts," he says simply. "I know my shit."

I turn to him, trying to keep the desperation from my voice. "I don't need a partner. I just need a loan."

"The money comes with me attached. I don't invest in a business blindly with no control. Please tell me you're not just another one of those fake friends only interested in my money."

"No! Of course not. I wouldn't even ask if I wasn't facing foreclosure."

He searches my expression. "Good."

It strikes me as even more important that I resist our chemistry. Crossing that line would make him think I'm using him. Why does he have to be the answer to my problem and the first man I've been drawn to in a very long time?

"So?" he prompts.

I stand, putting some distance between us. "I need to be full owner. It's my family's legacy."

He cocks his head. "So stubborn. Is that a family trait too?"

I ignore the taunt. I'm not bending on this ownership part. I walk to the fire, staring at the flickering flames. I know he's a good person deep down, or he wouldn't take such care with his sister. And his dog too! Look at her all pampered, curled up in her fluffy monogrammed bed. He brushed her little teeth! With the right negotiation, this could still work. I just don't know what I can offer in return.

"Where did you get Snowball?" I ask.

He glances over at Snowball. "Nice segue. So we're done talking about your desperate situation?"

I keep my eyes on Snowball because I'm sure Wyatt is smirking again. "I was just curious how you got such a cute little dog."

"Short version—the old woman who owned her died."

I turn to him. "I want the long version."

A ghost of a smile crosses his lips, and I'm drawn in all over again, crossing the room to sit next to him. It must just be the smirk that makes me crazy.

"She lived in the apartment under mine in the city. We used to see each other in the elevator a lot since she took Snowball on walks around the time I went out for lunch. I'd pet Snowball, and we'd talk a bit. Me and Mary Pat, I mean. Snowball can't talk." I laugh, and he grins. "One day I noticed Mary Pat wasn't there. She was frail, in her eighties, so I was concerned. I knocked on her door, and she told me she wasn't feeling well, so I offered to take Snowball on her walk. I was going out anyway, and a tiny dog like that doesn't need much of a walk. No big."

My heart squeezes. A generous man who doesn't want credit for what he did. "I'm sure she appreciated it."

"Yeah, that's what she said. The dog got used to me, I guess. And Mary Pat got weaker. I tried to get her to a doctor or at least contact family for her, but she refused. Later, I found out she had advanced lung cancer and was tired of hospitals. She always just said her body was worn out, and there was nothing anyone could do. I stopped by every day to feed and walk Snowball and check on Mary Pat. When she finally went to the hospital, I took Snowball to my place. And then I'm sure you can guess the end of the story. She died at the hospital a few days later."

"So sorry."

He nods. "She was a nice lady. I went to the funeral and tried to give Snowball to her son, who lived out in Oregon, but his apartment didn't allow pets, and he didn't want her anyway. Her daughter was up in Maine and already had six kids and two dogs. She didn't feel up to taking on another pet. They asked me to find Snowball a new home." He shrugs. "It wasn't a hard decision. She already had her stuff at my place."

My heart melts. "I love that story. A happy ending for Snowball. You know that's awesome what you did."

He rubs the back of his neck. "Snowball was used to me. What was I going to do, pawn her off on a stranger?"

He's a decent guy, reasonable and good-hearted. Suddenly I know what I can offer him. "That story made me realize what I can give you in return. Like you helped out your neighbor, I can help you out. How about this? You give me a loan, and I'll be on loan to you until my debt is paid. I can supervise contractors, walk your dog, whatever you need." I'm so pleased with my solution, which benefits both of us, I'm blindsided by his reply.

"Whatever I need? What if I said I need a lover?"

I gasp, speechless, even as my heart races with excitement.

He smirks. "Ha. Joking, and no, I'm partner or I'm out. Didn't we already go over that?"

I want to kick him. At the same time I want to kiss him.

What if he wasn't joking? Lover for hire? I mentally smack myself. *What are you thinking? You are not for sale.*

He gives me a slow sexy smile like he knows what I'm thinking and leans closer, murmuring, "Ah, Sydney, that look in your eyes is very telling."

A shiver runs down my spine. "I'm just thinking. You must be out, then. We're at a dead end." My voice sounds breathy.

His words run hot over my lips. "No professional relationship, then?"

A crackling moment of tension passes, my heartbeat pounding in my ears. If I cross this line, that's it. No chance of ever working together. Sex or business, want or need. Which pull is stronger? I can't think when he's this close. Everything's so mixed up in my mind.

"Wyatt," I whisper, "I can't."

He eases back from me. "Can't what?"

Can't kiss you. Can't work with you. Can't give up control in my business. I don't know which *can't* is most important anymore. My body hums with need as his gaze searches mine.

He gestures between us. "I'm confused. Is it that you don't want to work with me or—"

I grab his head and kiss him. Hard and quick, like I need to get it out of the way. I can't fight the impulse.

His response surprises me. He returns the kiss, his lips sliding in a caress that steals my breath before fitting more firmly against mine. He's tender yet sure like he was looking forward to this inevitability. His hand comes up to cup my jaw, his thumb stroking the sensitive spot just under my ear. My stomach flutters, sparks firing over my skin. I wrap my arms around his neck and go with it. Sensual heat floods me as his tongue explores. His hands stroke over my shoulders and down my back, resting low near my ass. Desire unfurls deep within me, a throbbing insistent beat.

He breaks the kiss, rubbing his thumb over my lower lip. "Sydney." He studies me, his demeanor relaxed but serious. "So..." He trails off like I'm supposed to fill in the blank.

I stare at his mouth, wanting more. Is it so wrong? It's not like we're doing business together. He offered to help me out under conditions I can't accept. So that means business is off the table.

He gives me a slow sexy smile. "What was that?"

"What?"

"You kissed me."

"You kissed me back."

"And?"

My brows draw together. "You know, you make every-thing aggravating and difficult."

He wraps a hand around the back of my neck and pulls me in close. "Why're the claws coming out?" He smirks as he strokes my hair back from my face.

He's entertained by me. *Fuck it.*

I kiss him again roughly, done playing games. He returns fire, his mouth demanding, his tongue tangling with mine. What started as a spark turns to a raging inferno of need. I reach for the end of his shirt and slide my hands underneath. My palms meet heated skin as they roam over tight abs and then broad chest. His hands slide over me from the nape of my neck to my sides, my hips, my ass. And then he's pulling me under him on the sofa, his thigh wedging between mine, bringing delicious friction. I throb with need, a dark craving for more.

I tug at his shirt, and he breaks the kiss, sitting up to pull it over his head. He's gorgeous, defined muscles with a smat-tering of chest hair disappearing in a faint line under his waistband. Pure lust rushes through me, and then I still, sensing someone staring. Big curious shih tzu eyes look back at me. Snowball wants to know what all this activity is about. I suddenly realize we're out in the open here in a room with no door. His sister is upstairs.

I put a hand to his chest just as he leans in for another kiss. "What about Kayla?"

"She's watching her favorite show with her earbuds in. Don't worry about her."

I push him off me, get up, and retrieve his shirt. "No can do." I toss his shirt at him. "We're out in the open here."

His shirt remains in his hand, his skin golden, the hard planes of his gorgeous body sorely tempting me. "Where's your sense of adventure?"

"I'm not into public sex."

"We were about to have sex? I thought it was a hot make-out session."

My cheeks flame. Oops. Guess we weren't on the same lusty journey. I don't usually move that fast, but the man has been tempting me for weeks, and I haven't been with anyone in way too long, and it was so *consuming* all I could think about was skin on skin, lusty satisfaction. Now would be a good time for me to slink out the door if we weren't trapped here in this snowstorm.

He pulls his shirt on. "I misunderstood, but I'm on board. Believe me. How about you get under the blanket while I run and grab a condom from my room?"

I eye the sofa, somewhere between lust and agitation.

He pulls me by my belt buckle until we're standing chest to chest, and wraps his arms around me. "Tell me exactly what the problem is, and I'll fix it."

I pull away, gesturing wildly. "This is not how I want to break my dry spell! On a sofa, where you'll probably pull a hamstring trying to fit, and there's potential witnesses! I'm sure Snowball will watch attentively too!" Snowball cocks her head at her name, watching me. "See? It's bad enough it's been ten months for me, and my ex couldn't get me off." I jam my hands on my hips, thinking about that. "Not entirely his fault. I told myself he was the kind of guy I *should* want, steady and responsible. He never got me worked up in *any way*, and that made for a nice comfortable relationship." I narrow my eyes at him. "Apparently, I prefer cocky guys who drive me crazy half the time!"

"Excellent. I'll just—"

"Hey, guys, what's up?" Kayla says, walking into the room with the laptop.

I drop my arms to my sides. *Thank God we're dressed.* "Not much. Just talking."

Wyatt shoots me an amused look.

"Do you want to watch a movie with me?" Kayla asks. "My show is making me too teary."

Wyatt's eyes go soft with sympathy. He shoots me a questioning look. He can't stand that she's teary. Even with sex on the table—I was still hoping to figure something out—he prioritizes his family. He's close with them. Just like me and my family.

"Sure, that sounds great," I tell Kayla, trying to sound civil. I'm both unreasonably irritated at the lust shutdown and mushy over the fact that Wyatt cares so much about his family.

Wyatt sends me an appreciative look. *Yeah, yeah, not like we're going to do anything out in the open here.* This is for the best. I was rushing things anyway. I just got worked up really fast. Lust doesn't usually make me unreasonable when thwarted.

The three of us settle on the sofa with Kayla in the middle. "This is great," she says, letting out a shaky breath. "I feel better already."

"Good," Wyatt says. "Now put on anything but a chick flick."

12

———

Wyatt

I keep sneaking glances over at Sydney while *Mamma Mia* plays. (Definitely a chick flick, I was overruled.) That kiss— intense, needy. Her sweet scent and something distinctly her was intoxicating. I knew it would be like that. The way we tangled verbally, I could always feel that tension.

As soon as business was out, I leaned in.

And *she* kissed *me*.

I usually take my time, never wanting to pressure a woman into the physical, so I was surprised when she started complaining about public sex. First kiss to sex? Hell yeah. If that's what she wants, I'm on board. I like her a lot and admire her grit. And I'm damn tired of flaky women who care more about what kind of car I drive than what I think. Not that Sydney agrees with everything I say, but she takes it seriously.

I catch her eye, and her lips part. *Yeah, she wants me.*

Business is business, and this is no longer that. No red flags. No conflict of interest. Just two consenting adults who've been circling each other for nearly two months now. Am I concerned about her debt? Yes. But she wants to do things her way, and I respect that. Some businesses are no longer viable, and it's important to know when to step back.

She's smart. She'll figure out what needs to happen. It just won't be with my help. And actually I'm glad. Now I don't have to worry she only wants me for my money.

Hold up. She's not using sex to get my money, is she? I hate that I even think that, but I've been burned too many times. I glance over at her again, and she smiles, a faint pink on her cheeks like she's remembering our hot kiss.

I face front. Okay, I'm not going to cut this short before giving her a chance. I'll be careful. Keep it casual. And if she turns around with her hand out, that's the end of it.

Even if I feel compelled to rescue her. Not this time. I've learned my lesson the hard way. In the meantime, why not enjoy what she's offering?

And she's Snowball approved. What more could I ask for? Ha.

As soon as the movie ends, I stand, clap my hands together, and rub them. "I'm beat. Time for bed. Who wants the bathroom first?" I look to my sister, hoping she'll take the hint to get ready and go to sleep so I can make my move. Sydney can't complain about being out in the open if Kayla's sleeping. And I'll dim the dining room light too. One could argue it's even romantic. As I will.

"I don't have a toothbrush or anything," Sydney says.

"Come with me," Kayla says. "I'll let you borrow my stuff. Well, not the toothbrush, you can use your finger for that."

They head upstairs together.

I look to Snowball sound asleep in her bed by the fire. She won't bother us. Still, I'd better take her out for one last whiz. I tamp down the last of the sparks in the fire, letting it die out.

A few minutes later, I'm outside freezing my ass off while Snowball stands on the snow, glaring at me.

"The faster you do your business, the faster you'll be back in bed."

She turns her back on me.

I'm not wearing my coat because I was in a hurry. I can feel my balls shriveling. "Do your business," I order.

She sniffs around and then gazes out to the woods, her ears perking up.

"Come on." I turn my back on an icy wind and turn back to her. "Yes, there's deer and other critters. You want your bed, right? Do your business."

Finally, she pees.

"Good girl! Good, good, good." I scoop her up and rush back inside. A full body shiver goes through me at the change in temperature. I set her back in her bed, grab the blanket off the sofa, and wrap it around me. The things I do for that dog.

I hear female laughter overhead. It's good they're getting along. I could never date someone my sisters hated. The family tension would be unbearable. My sisters wouldn't hesitate to share their opinion. Loudly.

I pace for a bit, keyed up, and then I arrange the pillow and blanket on the sofa for seduction under cover. One false move, and we'll roll right off. Hamstring pull is a distinct possibility. There's a few positions that would work, but it's not ideal. I'm used to having a king-size bed to work with. Too bad it's in storage.

A short while later, Sydney returns wearing my old gray Princeton T-shirt that hangs past her hips with a pair of Kayla's sweats that end at her calves. I normally sleep in my boxer briefs, so I don't have any sweats of my own to give her. She looks frigging adorable.

I walk over to her, checking her out. "The top half of you looks like you shrunk, and the bottom half looks like you're a giant. Very weird optical illusion going on here."

"Thank you," she says dryly. "Your turn in the bathroom."

"Sure." I lean close to whisper in her ear, "And then we'll finally be alone."

She backs up a step. "Uh, yeah, that's not happening."

I'm immediately suspicious of the female laughter I heard upstairs earlier. "Did Kayla say something about me?"

"Like what?"

"I don't know."

"Is there something I should know?"

"No." Other than Julia wrecked me and I haven't taken anyone seriously since. Besides, we already shared our war stories of horrible exes that claim to love you and then don't.

She narrows her eyes suspiciously.

I lift my palms. "Innocent."

"Hmm, I suppose if you had any dark secrets, you wouldn't confide them in your little sister. You coddle her."

"No, I take care of her."

"She's a full-grown woman."

"She's just going through a rough time. She needs me."

She tilts her head. "Tell me again why she gets your bed and you cram your six-foot-plus frame onto a sofa that she could easily fit on?"

"I told you she's having a hard time—" I gesture toward upstairs "—with the crying and everything. Anyone would be upset if their fiancé left them at the altar."

"Okay, but she says she's been here more than two weeks." She shrugs and fiddles with the bottom of my Princeton shirt. "Maybe you guys could switch places while she recovers, that's all."

A light goes on, and I read between the lines. She's saying sex is back on if we're together in my bed and Kayla's down here. But if I kick Kayla out for sex, then she won't want to go back to my room ever, and she'll be on the sofa for who knows how long. It's not ideal with the construction and all. I don't want her alone down here with a bunch of strange men working nearby. Yes, I'm overprotective. More so with her, she's the baby of the family.

"Goodnight, Wyatt," Sydney says pointedly.

I must've hesitated too long. "I got you." I turn and jog out of the room, heading upstairs.

"I have no idea what that means!" she calls out.

"Hold on!" I love the way she tangles with me. Most women go out of their way to agree with whatever I say—all soft tones—and I know it's because they're not in it for anything but themselves. What I can *give* to them.

I head to the bathroom to do the whole getting-ready ritual before going to my room. I knock.

"Come in," Kayla says. She's already tucked in bed, looking so young and fragile.

Okay, so I can't kick her out. Just look at her. On to plan B, seducing the pants off Sydney so she doesn't even notice we're on a sofa. Or maybe against the wall. That could work.

"Hey, just need to get something." I crouch down to my duffel bag in the corner and retrieve a strip of condoms from the box. Three is optimistic, but you never know.

"Wyatt!"

I toss the condoms back guiltily. "What?"

She sits up. "What are you doing?"

"Nothing. Go to sleep."

"I know what a condom looks like."

I grab them again, tuck them in my back pocket, and stand. "Well, uh, goodnight."

"Sydney says you're not together."

"Not yet. She wants to be."

"How do you know?"

She argued profusely for privacy. She wants me bad. "I just know."

She shakes her head. "Mom always said sex is better when you love someone."

I suppress my smart-ass response because I'd like her to believe that. "Mom's a smart lady."

Kayla's eyes are wide and earnest. "Do you love her?"

I point toward the door. "I really need to go. Do you have everything you need?"

She pats the bed. "Come here. Stop trying to race out the door. I'm worried about you. You've had nothing but terrible relationships for as long as I can remember."

I hang my head, knowing she's not going to let this go. Sisters can talk you to death. I sit on the edge of the mattress. "Don't worry. Sydney's Snowball approved." I think about Sydney's strong and feisty nature, how devoted she is to preserving her family legacy, and that reminds me to be wary. I don't know how far she'll go to save her restaurant.

"Have you been on a real date?"

"A few." If you count me showing up at her restaurant for months, and us bantering for hours. The way she slapped her ass at me was one of my favorite times.

"Okay, that's a good start. I do think Mom is right. That's why I'm waiting for marriage."

I blink. She's waiting for marriage. A twenty-four-year-old virgin. My mind immediately goes to the guy who left her at the altar. I bet he wanted to marry her so he could finally have sex, but then couldn't go through with getting shackled. Crap. I can't say any of that.

"Wyatt?"

"Good for you."

She grips her hands tightly together and says in a small voice, "I think, in hindsight, that might be why Rob was so eager to marry me."

Rob. I've finally got a first name. PhD. Same university. Now I can narrow it down, track him, and kick his ass. "If that's the reason, you're better off without him." That was definitely the reason. Why else would he want to marry her so quick and then bail?

She sighs. "I know."

I stand. "Okay. I'm going to—"

"I'm thinking it's a mistake to wait. Do you think I screwed up?"

I consider my words carefully. I don't want her to feel any worse than she already does. "You should just do what feels right for you. If that's waiting for marriage, then that's what you should do."

She twists her lips to the side. "I guess not waiting hasn't worked out any better for you."

"Sex and love don't always go together. For me they don't."

She slowly shakes her head. "Maybe you should take Mom's advice and wait for love, and I should do the opposite, so men aren't dying to marry me just to get some."

I open my mouth and shut it again. I'm out of my league with the frank little-sister sex talk, and the last thing I want is to give her bad advice. "Think on it some more. Maybe check in with Paige or Brooke." Sisterly advice would be much better in this situation.

She frowns. "They don't believe in waiting. They say

Mom doesn't know what she's talking about because she married young, and I'm missing out."

"Hmm, really? Huh." I'm drowning in deep awkward water. Mom's the one who handled the sex talk. I don't even like to *think* about my sisters having sex, or not having sex, but still talking about it. *Can I go now?*

Kayla continues. "They say Mom only said that so we wouldn't end up pregnant and drop out of school."

Probably true. Our mom is smart like that. For me, she put a box of condoms in my room when I got my first girlfriend in high school, Tara, and told me to keep it covered. Which I did. Never once did Mom mention sex and love in the same sentence. That seems like a double standard. Maybe she thought I was in love. I was mostly in love with sex, though I did *like* Tara. A lot. She let me have sex with her.

I pat Kayla on the head, which she hates. "Good talk. Night."

Kayla gets out of bed and rips off the blanket. Sheets come off next. *Awesome. She's giving me the bed.* She tosses the blanket back and grabs a pillow, tucking the sheets under one arm.

"I'll take the sofa," she says. "Go ahead and make the bed with your stuff. Sydney and I will have a sleepover. We can both fit on the sofa, sleeping head to toe." She heads for the door.

"Or…"

She grins at me over her shoulder. "I'll give her the option."

~

Sydney

I settle on the sofa, using Wyatt's pillow and blanket, watching Snowball curled up in her cozy bed. I left the overhead dining room light on dim so Wyatt could find his way back. I just know I'm going to end up crammed on this sofa with him because I can't resist the pull. I've had a taste of him, and I've been aching with desire ever since. I never knew I could ache for someone. I know I said it's not happening, but my body says differently despite his sister upstairs, this room with no door, and us cramming onto a sofa. I even put my jeans back on for a sexier look. (Kayla's sweatpants were *not* flattering.) Once we get the lust out of our system, I'll have to sleep on top of him to fit, or kick him off the sofa entirely. The things I think about when I'm blindsided by lust.

"Hi."

I scramble to sit up on the sofa, surprised to see Kayla. Thank God I didn't get naked! She's holding a pillow and sheets. Did he send his sister downstairs to sleep with me? I thought Wyatt was just as caught up in lust as I was. "Where's Wyatt?"

"I gave him back his bed. I felt bad he was on the floor down here."

I'm ridiculously disappointed. "Oh."

She smiles. "I thought we could have a sleepover." She perches on the arm of the sofa. "I could take the floor, or we could sleep head to toe on the sofa. Neither of us is that big, so I think it would work. We could stay up late for girl talk like I do with my sisters."

"Girl talk," I echo. It's not like I never had sleepovers with my girl friends, but, dammit, I thought Wyatt wanted to be with me. He sends his sister without even a goodnight kiss! Unacceptable.

I get off the sofa. "Thanks, but you can have the sofa. I need to go talk to your brother."

She nods. "Okay. Just one thing. He's had a lot of crappy relationships. You should only be with him if you care for him. You don't have to love him yet, but think about it, okay? He's worth it."

I blink a few times, not sure what to say. I've been driven by my lust, and now she's bringing it into emotional territory. I can't imagine Wyatt and I working out long term the way we push each other's buttons. And, while I don't normally go for casual flings, I'm here and I need this.

"Got it," I finally say.

"Goodnight."

"Night."

I go upstairs and peek in the open door of Wyatt's room. He's smoothing out a blue plaid blanket on top of the bed. He turns, a slow smile spreading across his face. "You chose me."

I shut the door behind me. "Versus a sleepover with your sister?"

"Yeah. She said she'd give you the option to sleep with me or her."

I shake my head. "You guys are so weird. I came up here because you didn't even say goodnight." I gesture toward downstairs. "Just left me with your sister."

He smirks. "Are you cross with me again, Cindy?" I suddenly realize it's his way of being funny—the smirk, the old-fashioned word *cross*, calling me the wrong name.

I play along, lifting my chin like I really am angry when all I want is to tangle up close and personal. "Yes."

He walks toward me, a predatory look in his eyes. A rush of lust makes my entire body heat in anticipation of impact.

13

—————

He boxes me in against the door, his palms on either side of my head. "And you came up here to read me the riot act on good manners?"

"Yeah." My voice comes out breathy.

He smirks, leaning in close, his words running hot over my lips. "You want me."

"Yes."

His lips meet mine in a scorching kiss, reminding me exactly what I came here for—passion. The thing I've been missing out on my whole life and never knew it, until him. He tastes minty, smells woodsy fresh, and feels wonderful, his hard body pressing against mine. He kisses me like he has all night. And we do, here in this timeless place with the storm trapping us overnight and late tomorrow. *Tomorrow.*

I break the kiss. "How's this going to go afterward?"

His hand comes up to cup my jaw, stroking my cheek. I lean into it, loving his touch, not too soft, just right, firm and sure. "What do you mean?"

I put my hand on his, pulling it down from my cheek so I can focus. "I can't deal with an awkward morning after. I'm not sure how long I'll be stuck here. It could be late afternoon." It's both a warning and a worry. If it's casual, I'd normally want to leave as soon as possible.

He nuzzles my neck, working his way up to my ear. "Poor Sydney. You might actually have to face your lover in the morning."

"And his sister."

He lifts his head, his whiskey eyes meeting mine intently. "We'll have sex in the morning too. That way it's not awkward. And when I finally finish with you, you'll be limp and barely able to lift a finger, let alone utter a peep of discontentment."

My breath shudders out. "That's a big promise."

He locks the door behind me, the snick of the lock signaling it's *on*. "I can deliver. And if my sister asks, tell her you care for me. She's sentimental about these things."

I stare at him. We're so close we're breathing the same air. That must be why I'm light-headed. Then I realize he told me that to warn me it's just casual. He's not sentimental about sex is what he's really saying. Looks like we're in agreement —long term we'd end up killing each other.

"Just casual sex." My voice comes out louder than I meant it to. "Good."

He nips my lower lip. "So let's get to the good stuff." He moves so quick I don't have time to react, scooping me up, cradled in his arms. He sets me down on the bed and covers me with his body, a ghost of a smile crossing his lips before his mouth crashes down over mine. Gone is the slow, all-night kisses, and this, this rough plundering is exactly what I need. I widen my legs, welcoming him in close. Desire floods me as we fit together, the ache returning, needing him to fill me.

I slide my hand through his thick hair, loving the feel of it, loving the weight and heat of him on top of me. He holds my jaw as his mouth claims mine, his soft beard rubbing against me. The kiss goes on and on, urgent and wild, my hips rocking mindlessly under him, silently asking for more.

He sits back on his heels and pulls his shirt off. I immediately sit up to explore, roaming my hands all over him.

"Hold up," he says, out of breath. He pulls his phone from his pocket and taps it a few times. "I have the feeling you're going to be loud." A moment later, a slow sexy song plays. He sets the phone on top of a cardboard box that seems to serve as a nightstand.

I purse my lips. "Let me guess, your sex playlist."

"I hit shuffle." He curls his hand around the back of my neck and kisses me long and deep. "Your turn." He pulls my shirt off and undoes the front clasp of the bra. "Beautiful," he says reverently, pushing me back onto the mattress.

I sigh as he kisses a hot trail from my collarbone to my breast, stopping to nibble and taste on his way. His beard rubs against me, adding to the sensation. He kisses round and round my breast before drawing my nipple into his mouth. My breath stutters out at the firm wet tug, a direct line of pleasure to my sex. I throb against my jeans, my fingers tangling in his hair. Sensation coils inside me, tight and hot.

"Wyatt," I gasp out, "I need the jeans off. Everything."

He releases my nipple with a lingering taste and looks up at me. "All in good time." Then he kisses my other breast, making his slow way round and round. I'm about to protest I need him too much for slow when his hand slides down to undo my jeans button and zipper. *Yes!* His fingers slip under my panties, and I nearly cry with relief.

"You're so wet," he says, sliding his hand out of my panties and putting his finger in his mouth to taste.

My breath catches, and then suddenly I'm wild with need. I push him off me enough to yank my jeans and panties down over my hips. I struggle to get them off, but I can't do it with him hovering over me. "Off," I order.

He smirks. "Me or the jeans?"

"Wyatt!"

"*Someone* is demanding. Ten months must feel like a *really* long time to go without."

I clamp my mouth shut. It probably hasn't been that long for him.

He pulls my jeans and panties all the way off and tosses them on the floor. I reach for him, but he stays just out of reach, kneeling at my feet. He strokes up my calves, sliding slowly up my legs. "Why'd you wait so long, Sydney? You're beautiful, smart, fiery. Any guy would want you."

My eyes get hot. That was so sweet, and I don't want to admit the truth. Because then it sounds like I was crushed by my ex saying he didn't love me anymore, when I was really just busy working and stuff. I don't know what to say, so I don't say anything. Instead I move further into the bed, hoping he'll take the hint and join me.

He crawls over me and kisses me. "Okay. All the more reason to take my time." His mouth leaves a hot trail from my throat all the way down to my hip, where he lingers. His big hands slide up the inside of my thighs, and then he surprises me, pushing my leg up and kissing the back of my knee. I suck in air. It's exquisitely sensitive there. No one's ever kissed me in that spot.

"So sensitive," he croons, kissing his way up the inside of my leg.

My fingers grip the sheets. I know where this is going, and I want it. Desperately.

He kisses my hip, and then the crease of my leg, flicking his tongue over it, teasing. "I need to taste you."

"Yes. Taste me."

His fingers slide between my legs, parting me gently, before he dips his head and takes one long lick.

My breath shudders out. "More."

"Just getting started," he murmurs, the words vibrating and hot against my most sensitive area.

"Yes," I say on a sigh. And then there are no words. Pleasure floods me as he takes expert control. I completely let go as he guides me slowly, languidly up an ever-spiraling pleasure ride. My hips rock of their own accord, lost in bliss. My fingers run through his hair, holding him to me, and then suddenly I'm gripping his hair as his mouth turns hungry.

"Ah, ah, ah," I chant, louder and louder, shocked at the intensity as I race to release. His fingers thrust inside me at the same time as he gently sucks, and I explode with a startled cry. Pleasure rockets through me, electric waves radiating out from my core all the way to my scalp and down to my toes. He stays with me, prolonging the pleasure, slow and easy, until I go limp with a sigh.

I place a hand on his gorgeous, wonderful head. "Thank you."

He smiles. "You're welcome, beautiful. My pleasure." He kisses his way up my body, and I wrap my arms around him. Then I widen my legs, totally ready for part two.

He sucks my lower lip. "Hold up." He slides a strip of condoms out from under the pillow.

I prop up on an elbow, watching him rip open the packet. "Nice hiding spot."

"I didn't want to be too forward and have them waiting on the pillow, staring you in the face with *expectations*." He winks. "Kidding. I was hiding them in case of a different visitor." He rolls it on and returns to me, guiding himself in slowly.

I tilt my hips, drawing him in further, and wrap my legs high up around his waist. He's thick, making me ache even more. It's been way too long.

He groans and entwines our fingers together, gazing into my eyes. "You feel amazing."

"You too. More. Harder."

He thrusts fully inside, and we both moan. He starts a slow rhythm, kissing me at the same time, but I need more. I nip his lower lip hard enough to make him gasp.

He lifts his head, his eyes smoldering into mine. "More, huh?"

I nod. He releases my hands, and I instantly stroke over the hard planes of his back, loving the leashed power there. His hand slides between us, stroking me rapidly as he pumps into me.

"Yes, yes, yes," I chant.

He bites my neck, and I moan. "You're a talker. I knew it."

I laugh, and then I pant as pleasure coils tight inside me. "I never was before," I gasp out. "You're good."

He watches me intently, rocking into me, his fingers wicked. "I'm awesome."

"You are," I say, my voice hitting a high note. "I'm—"

"I know." His mouth covers mine, swallowing my cry as my climax roars through me. I rock helplessly against him, my body contracting around him. He swears, pushes my thigh up, opening me further as he thrusts hard and fast. Shockwaves of white-hot pleasure steal my breath. He groans, his head arching with his own release as he pumps into me. I moan softly, every movement rocketing more pleasure through me. Finally, he releases my leg and gives me his weight.

I work on catching my breath. Slowly, reality returns. I just had sex with a man I'm really starting to like. The same man who used to make me crazy. This could be dangerous. He gets under my skin so easily, both in good and bad ways.

Please don't make it awkward. He swore it wouldn't be, but all the thoughts crowding my brain are making it hard for me to relax.

He lifts his head. "Oh no you don't." He rolls off me and turns me so I'm on my side, and he's spooning me from behind. "You, my chatty sex queen, are not going to have the energy for freaking out."

Sex queen? Me? I'm too flattered for speech.

His voice rumbles by my ear, bringing a delicious shiver. "I felt you tense up, saw the look of sheer panic." He lifts my leg up and over his. "Nope. Not having it after all my good work."

I can't believe he read me so easily. "I was just—" The breath whooshes from my body as his fingers delve between my legs, shocking me into silence. My back arches against him, his touch too intense too soon. And then he gentles, moving in slow circles, and my mind shuts down. Pleasure clouds my brain; my entire body relaxes, knowing he'll take me where I need to go.

"God, I love feeling you let go," he says gruffly.

"You earned it."

He nips my earlobe, his fingers stilling. "I earned your trust?"

"You earned my orgasm with your competence."

"And you just earned a bonus orgasm."

"Yes, please."

He chuckles darkly and then makes good on his promise. Once. Twice. By the third time, I'm trembling all over, begging for release.

"Hang on," he growls. "Not yet."

I pant, beyond words, my body arching with need, my fingers digging into his shoulder behind me. He sucks on my neck and increases his rhythm, and I break violently, shuddering as pleasure floods me. Long moments later, I collapse, completely limp.

He kisses my temple and sets my leg down. "Better. I like you limp and content." He gets out of bed and tucks the blanket around me. "I'll be back in a few for the next round."

I groan, way too sated for any more. *So sleepy.* I can't seem to get the words out.

I hear the door shut behind him and close my eyes. I'm asleep instantly.

～

Wyatt

The next morning, I slip out of bed to take Snowball out and feed her. Then I put her dog bed next to the sofa so she can be with Kayla. I got a message from the crew chief that they won't be in today. The roads aren't passable. Good by me because now I get Sydney all to myself.

I head upstairs just as Sydney's coming out of the bathroom. She must've brushed her hair because when I left the bed this morning, it was wild and rumpled. I might've had something to do with that. I bet she brushed her teeth in preparation for more sex with me. How do I know she wants more? Her eyes are eating me up in the long-sleeved shirt and jeans I threw on, and she's only wearing my Princeton T-shirt. If she was done with the sex part of our day, she'd be fully dressed.

She lifts a hand in awkward greeting. "Uh, hi. I didn't know where you went."

"Took care of the dog." I gesture toward the bedroom. "After you."

She blushes, rubbing the side of her neck, where she has beard burn. "Is this weird?"

I close the distance and grab her, chomping down the side of her neck. She squeals in surprise. I give her ass a pat. "Time for bed, troublemaker."

She walks back into my room, smiling. "I'm a troublemaker? No, sir! You're—"

I make a he-man groan and scoop her up, tossing her on the bed. She just laughs and opens her arms to me. A rush of affection floods me at the sight. I'm tempted to hug her and hold her close, but I remember the rules of this game. Casual. It's the safest route.

I rip my clothes off and then do the same to hers, climbing on top of her and pinning her wrists to the mattress.

"I want to be on top this time," she says.

"You have to earn it."

She rocks her hips into me, smiling wickedly. "I will, trust me."

I roll to my back and pull her on top of me. "You're going to torture me, aren't you?" I ask in mock horror.

"No more than you tortured me."

I groan. I definitely drew out her orgasms and then pushed for more. She's going to be positively evil.

Her hands roam down my chest, followed by her mouth, nipping and licking. By the time she reaches my rock-hard erection, I stop breathing. Her hand closes around the base, and then her mouth takes me in.

Her eyes meet mine, gleaming, and I nearly lose it right there. She begins the torture with one long suck. I fist a hand in her hair as though I have any control. I'm already halfway there as her mouth works up and down.

I groan long and low. There's nothing but her hot wet mouth and an intense tightening pleasure, ratcheting up, up, up.

"Wait," I gasp. "I want to be inside you." I reach for the last condom under the pillow.

Shockingly, she releases me, giving me a sexy smile. "I want that too."

As soon as the condom's on, she climbs up my body and impales herself on me. *Fuck.* I grip her hips tightly, needing to control it, slow it down.

She moans softly as I move her slow and steady. She grips my shoulders, her eyes closed with her pleasure.

"So beautiful," I murmur.

Her eyes open, gazing into mine, an intensely intimate moment that takes me by surprise. Like we're recognizing the real person under the defenses. I swallow hard, overwhelmed by the rush of emotion, my hands still in a tight grip on her hips.

Her eyes go soft. "Wyatt, more."

I loosen my grip on her hips, and she's instantly riding me. Faster and faster. Her beautiful breasts bouncing, her breath coming in harsh pants. I'm lost in a flood of pleasure and need. Her urgency becomes mine, and I know I can't hang on much longer. She shouts my name as she climaxes, her body tightening around me rhythmically. I grab her hips, pump into her once more, and then I explode, pleasure spearing through me.

She lies down on top of me, and I hold her tight, spent. She feels so good in my arms.

A few moments later, she lifts her head. "Was I too loud?"

I laugh. "No sex music to cover it up."

She smacks my chest. "I knew that was your sex playlist!"

"Yes, you were too loud. Just like now."

She lowers her voice. "Do you think she heard?"

"I'm sure she did. She can hear the mailman from a mile away."

Her brows knit together in confusion.

I run a finger down her nose. "Dogs are known for their excellent hearing."

She narrows her eyes. "You know that's not who I meant."

"My sister is sleeping, and the crew can't make it here today with the road conditions."

She traces a circle on my chest. "So that means…"

I run a hand over her silky hair. "Yes, you may pleasure me for hours."

She grins. "This isn't as awkward as I thought it'd be, you know, after."

"That's because I won't let it be." I roll her under me and kiss her, stroking her hair back from her face. God, she's beautiful. "And if you give me any awkward trouble later, you'll find yourself right back here. Is that what you want? 'Cause that's what I want."

She smiles, and I kiss that smiling mouth. *As long as we're in bed, everything's perfect. I hope the storm goes on for a week.*

14

———

Sydney

I'm feeling all warm and content, something I never thought I'd be around the man formerly known as Satan. If I hadn't gotten to know him on his own turf, I don't think I'd have stopped being furious long enough to notice the good heart hiding under his smirky demeanor. He smirks when he thinks something's funny. And clearly he found sparring with me *wildly* entertaining. There was no malice in it. I just took it personally because it's my sore spot—my family's legacy on my shoulders, a failing restaurant, all that stuff I'm trying not to think about right now. I just want to enjoy the moment.

I sigh and rest my head on my hand, leaning over the kitchen island, watching as he makes me breakfast. He put two Eggo waffles in the toaster, and now he's microwaving breakfast sausage.

He serves up my breakfast a few moments later. "Bet you didn't know your excellent lover was also an excellent cook."

I fight back my impulse to jokingly say he cooks like he makes love—fast and easy. I am so bad. He really was awesome. I take a bite of waffle instead.

He wraps a hand around the back of my neck and squeezes. "Don't think I didn't notice that smart-ass remark you were holding back."

I chew and swallow. "Who, me?"

He kisses me. "Yeah, you, my fiery she-devil."

"Ha! I used to secretly call you Satan."

He grins. "Then we're well matched."

"Isn't this cozy?" Kayla says cheerily, walking into the kitchen. She's still wearing the faded red sweatshirt and sweatpants she slept in.

I instantly flush. "Morning."

Wyatt hauls me against his side and offers me his sausage, like actually trying to feed it to me. *Phallic symbol, anyone?* I glare at him, and he smirks.

Kayla is thankfully oblivious as she gets an Eggo waffle from the freezer and puts it in the toaster.

I wrench away from him and take a delicate bite of waffle, working on looking like this is all super normal. *Just the morning after having sex with your brother!*

Kayla helps herself to a glass of water before turning to me. "Guess my sweats weren't comfortable, huh?"

I'm wearing his oversized Princeton T-shirt and his basketball shorts. "They were a little small on me."

Her lips twitch. "Uh-huh."

I turn to Wyatt, my cheeks flushing. He swore this wouldn't be awkward, and it feels more awkward by the minute. He pulls my head close and kisses my temple. "Doesn't she look adorable in my stuff?" he asks Kayla over my head. "The good news is that Sydney's in love with me, so everything's cool."

I nearly choke on my own spit. I want to deny it, but he smirks, and I realize he's just trying to lighten the mood.

"Yup," I say, going back to my breakfast. "Good thing too because he worships me. It's disgustingly cute."

Kayla claps. "Oh, Wyatt! I'm so happy for you! After Jul—"

"You know what?" Wyatt says, pressing a finger to his lips. "You should stay on the sofa from now on, Kayla."

"Ah," she says, a knowing look in her eyes. "Got it. No problem." She grabs her waffle with a napkin and gets her glass of water. "Sounds like I'll be seeing a lot more of you, Sydney." She smiles and turns to go.

"Set your alarm for seven a.m. sharp," Wyatt calls after her. "I don't want you downstairs alone when the crew gets to work."

She stiffens and turns back. "I'm sure it's fine." She turns on her heel and walks off to the sofa room.

"Was that an agreement?" he calls after her.

No response.

"Why?" I ask him.

He keeps his eyes locked on where she just left for the sofa room. "Because Kayla's in a vulnerable state, and I don't want her to deal with unwanted attention from strange men."

"Are they creeps?" I ask.

He scowls. "They're fine. Just not for Kayla."

"What's wrong, Beelzebub?" I ask.

He cracks a smile and pulls me close, nuzzling into my neck, kissing the sensitive spot behind my ear, bringing a shiver. "Nothing."

I pull back to look at him. "Is it a problem that your grown-ass sister doesn't want you telling her when to wake up and that she has to hide upstairs while the crew's here?"

"Can you believe it? Normally she'd be hanging upstairs in my room anyway, so what's the difference?"

"Hmm, what could it be? She doesn't like being bossed by her big brother?"

His gaze drops to my mouth, and he brushes his thumb over my lower lip, pressing on it. Next thing I know, we're kissing, breakfast forgotten. He lifts me by the waist and sets me on top of the island.

He pushes my legs wider and pulls me close so we're all lined up. Heat pools between my legs. His hands slip under my T-shirt, running up my sides. "You're addicting."

A hot shiver races through me. "I'm not sure this is a good idea." Then I kiss him again. The pull is too strong.

"Forgot my vitamin!" Kayla sings as she walks in.

I jerk back, startled.

Wyatt doesn't move, his hands resting on my sides very

close to my breasts. I push them down, and he holds me by the hips instead. "Did you really, runt?" he says over my shoulder to Kayla. "Or are you pissed at me for telling you to steer clear of the crew?"

"I'm sure if I made even a peep of irritation, you'd come running," she returns, getting a vitamin from the cabinet.

He frowns. "It's for your own protection. Emotional and otherwise."

She rolls her eyes, muttering under her breath as she walks away, "Not like I have any interest in guys right now, geez."

Wyatt turns and yells after her, "They have interest in you!"

"Little heavy-handed there," I say.

He shakes his head, lowering his voice. "She's a mess right now. Plus she's a virgin."

I shove his chest. "No! She told you that?"

"Yeah, she tells me all kinds of stuff I don't want to hear. She's waiting for marriage as our mom told her to."

"How old is she?"

"Twenty-four."

"Wow."

"Yeah." He wraps my hair around his fist. "How old were you for your first time?"

I make a face. "You don't want to know."

"Course I do. That's why I asked."

"How old were you?"

"Seventeen."

I look at a point over his shoulder, slightly embarrassed that I was younger. I don't know why I'm embarrassed. It was consensual, and we were in a relationship. "Sixteen, but I was almost seventeen."

He pinches my chin. "It's all good whatever you did in the past. I only care about right now."

I wrap my arms around his neck, smiling. "Good."

"Did you like it?"

"Like what?"

"Sex with your high school boyfriend?"

I think about that. Crammed into the back seat of his car, the rush of heat, and then over too quick. "Kinda. I didn't know any differently. It was fine."

"For me it was awesome, though I suspect less so for her. I wasn't the lover you see today."

I hook my ankles behind his back. "And that's all I care about right now."

He picks me up, plastered against his front. "Going back upstairs."

I laugh and wave toward our half-eaten breakfast. "What about our waffles?"

He nips my neck. "I'll whip up a fresh batch."

"Why did you tell Kayla I'm in love with you?"

He starts climbing the stairs, not at all winded by carrying me with him. "She believes sex and love should go together and told me to wait until there was love. Clueless virgin."

I laugh, but it sounds hollow.

He sets me down at the top of the stairs, his large hand cradling my jaw, his whiskey eyes searching mine. I throw my arms around his neck and kiss him passionately. We have this, and I need it. That has to be enough.

He guides me back toward his bedroom, never breaking the kiss, and we stumble through the doorway, slamming the door behind us.

Am I crazy? After complaining to anyone who'll listen that the man is Satan, I now like being with him so much I don't even want to go home. It's kinda embarrassing.

We haven't had one argument since we first had sex. Was that the problem? Just a buildup of sexual tension? Or is it the fact that we haven't talked much beyond sharing our history? I guess I'll find out. He told me to stop by tonight after work. I finish work at midnight. Yeah, it's a booty call, but hell, the sex is phenomenal. If that's all it is, I'm sure it'll burn out soon enough. Why not enjoy it in the meantime?

Though there are times, when his eyes meet mine with such warmth, I just melt.

I call Drew later that morning to see how it is out there. I'm hoping I can get home *with* my car, but I'll deal without it if I have to. I'm sure the tree guys will be busy for days.

He answers, sounding out of breath. "Hey, Syd. A tree fell on my garage. I've got Adam over here with his chainsaw, helping me clear it."

"Is your truck okay?"

"Yeah, the tree damaged the roof but didn't break through. Eli says Route 15 is clear."

"Okay, I'll call someone else for a ride."

"Hold on." I hear him talking to our brother in the background. "Adam's almost done here. He'll get to you next and clear the tree blocking your car. Then you're home free."

"Great, thanks." I say bye and head to the sofa room, where Wyatt's sitting on the sofa. Kayla's upstairs. "Adam's stopping by soon with his chainsaw to clear the tree, and then I'll go."

"Why the long face?"

I paste on a smile. "I'm happy." It's ridiculous to be sad about our magical time ending. I should just be glad we had this. And if it doesn't go much further, it just wasn't meant to be.

He crooks his finger at me. I walk over and sit next to him.

He hauls me into his lap, tucking me sideways. I lean my head against his chest with a sigh. "You'll miss me." He shifts, meeting my eyes. "Go ahead and admit it. You don't want to leave because I'm the best lover you ever had, and you hate the idea of going to work."

I laugh but admit nothing. "I haven't had stress relief like this in forever."

He chuckles. "I could slash your tires so you have to stay even longer. Would that help?"

I push his shoulder. "Psycho."

He gazes at me warmly, and a bubble of pure happiness rises in me. "I'll miss you too."

~

A short while later, Adam arrives. Wyatt answers the door, Snowball in tow, and I follow him. Adam's wearing a dark gray wool cap over his short brown hair, black fleece jacket, jeans, and work boots. He's tall, wiry with muscle, and reserved. A lone-wolf type. He works for himself mostly, only using help from a father and son team for bigger jobs.

"Adam," Wyatt says warmly, "thanks for coming to the rescue. I don't have any axes or chainsaws hiding in my lighthouse."

Adam cracks a smile. "Right." He jerks his chin at me. "Glad to see you in one piece. That tree came damn close."

"I know. It was terrifying."

He jerks his thumb toward the door. "I'm going to get to work. Just wanted to let you know I'm here. Once I get the tree in pieces, I'd appreciate some help getting it out of the way. Do you mind if I come back for the wood with a couple of my guys and my van? It's a fine tree."

"All yours, man," Wyatt says. "I want to see what you do with it." He turns to me. "Your brother is a true artisan."

Adam ducks his head, embarrassed by the compliment, and walks outside.

I smile at Wyatt. "I think so too. Did you visit his workshop?"

"Yup. And I went through his online portfolio too. That's why I hired him."

"He made an awesome tree house for his neighbor when he was between jobs. I would've loved it as a kid."

"I saw that, with the shutters for the windows and the skylight. Like I said, a true artisan."

I beam, proud of my brother. "I'll thank you on his behalf. He doesn't do well with compliments. I think he holds his work to a higher standard."

"Every artist does."

~

Once the tree is cleared, I know my time is up. I push down the feeling of dread. Back to work at the place that's sinking around me and pulling me down with it. "I need to grab my purse," I say. We're still outside.

Wyatt turns to Adam. "You want to come in for coffee?"

"Sure."

I gape for a moment before following them inside. Adam must like Wyatt. He's normally the kind to do his job and go. He doesn't linger for coffee and conversation. My defenses crumble a little more. Adam-approved means something. He only lets people in he believes are trustworthy.

The two of them are in deep conversation about the possibilities for the pine tree. Wyatt's asking how difficult it would be to make rocking chairs out of it for his porch.

"It's the ideal wood for that," Adam says and then launches into a surprisingly detailed explanation about why.

Wyatt gets the coffeemaker started. I take a seat at the island with Adam. Snowball goes up on her hind legs, sniffing Adam's boots madly. She probably smells his bulldog's slobber on them. Adam reaches down, absently rubbing her behind the ears as he talks.

Once Adam winds down his rhapsody on pine, Wyatt says, "I'd like to commission some rocking chairs, then. Unless you wanted to use the wood for yourself."

"I'll take a piece, but there's plenty to go around."

"What were you thinking of making with it before I rudely claimed rocking chairs? Four, please."

Adam smiles. *Another smile!* "I like to let the wood speak to me. What does it want to be?"

"So Zen," I quip.

Adam arches a brow.

"I told you he was an artisan," Wyatt says. "He approaches it like a sculptor. I can't wait until you get started on my library. Next week, right?"

"On my schedule."

A few minutes later, Wyatt serves up coffee and stands across from us at the island. "How bad is it out there?"

I take a sip of coffee.

Adam wraps his hand around the mug. "Highway department cleared the main roads. Some of the side roads have downed branches still, but you can get around them."

I fill Adam in on the reality of the lighthouse being a water tower, but it turns out he already knew from Wyatt. I guess they talked quite a bit before. I had no idea.

Kayla walks in. "Mmm, fresh coffee." She halts, looking past me to my brother, her brown eyes widening. Her cheeks flush, and she raises a hand to self-consciously smooth her hair down. She has major bed head, and she's still in her faded red sweatshirt and baggy sweatpants. "I didn't know we had company."

"Didn't you hear the chainsaw?" Wyatt asks.

Kayla can't stop staring at Adam. My brother seems equally transfixed.

I make the introductions.

"Hi," Adam says, offering his hand.

Kayla gives him a quick handshake, blushing furiously. "Nice to meet you. I don't usually look like I just rolled out of bed. Obviously. People get dressed. But, uh, see you." She bolts.

A smile plays over Adam's lips as he watches her go.

Wyatt gestures to where Kayla just went upstairs. "I'd apologize for my sister, but you've got a sister. You know the drill."

"I'd never apologize for wearing sweats," I say. "Someone comes into my house and they don't like the way I'm dressed, that's their problem."

"Yes, well, Kayla's not a she-devil," Wyatt says with a smirk.

Adam's brows rise in question.

I shake my head. "I call him Satan. Sometimes Beelzebub."

"Term of endearment," Wyatt says. "She's crazy about me."

Adam turns to me, a question in his eyes.

I wave absently. "He's crazy about me is the real truth." I point at Wyatt. "Ha."

He grins. "You really know how to wound a guy."

Adam stands. "I'd better get going. Syd, you want me to wait to be sure your car's all right getting out of here, or are you good?"

"I'm good. Thanks for your help."

He nods once, looks toward the stairs, and heads out. Snowball trails after him, followed by Wyatt. I hear the door shut behind them and sigh. Now it's really time to go.

Kayla pokes her head downstairs, her hair now brushed smooth, fully dressed in a sweater and leggings. "Did Adam leave already?"

"Yeah, but don't worry, he'll be back next week to work on the library. He's a master carpenter. You can stare your fill."

She smooths a hand through her already smooth hair. "I wasn't staring, was I? Oh God. So embarrassing. I was just surprised! I didn't know we had company." She mutters to herself, heading back upstairs.

"He's single!" I call.

She turns back. "I'm not looking for a guy! He just seemed nice."

"You got that from *hi*?"

She turns on her heel without another word.

15

———

Three weeks later…

Wyatt

I can hardly believe how easy things are with Sydney after our rocky start. We never fight now. She practically lives at my place. My parents were a fast and furious romance, living together after only a month. Sydney says her dad proposed to her mom on their first date. Sometimes that's how it goes. All I know is I'm happier than I've been in a very long time. Still, I'm cautious. I've been burned too many times by women who want something from me, and if anyone needs to take, it's Sydney. Her money troubles are a constant source of stress. She doesn't want to do business with me, and now that we're involved, I agree it's best not to.

I'm in the parking lot of her restaurant to pick her up for our date. She took a rare Thursday night off for it. I'm taking her to a cool Mexican-Jewish restaurant in the city. The instant she gets into my car, the scent of honeysuckle and sexy woman wraps around me. I know her perfume now, honeysuckle. Lust rushes through my veins. I can't resist kissing her.

She smiles and pulls a silver gift bag out of her giant purse. "Got you something."

I stare at it, my throat unexpectedly tight. It's the first time a woman has given me anything in *years*. Women *always* want something from me, expensive jewelry mostly, sometimes shopping trips or luxury getaways. They ask and ask, take and take. Sydney's asked for nothing, and now she's giving me a present. *Giving*, not taking.

My voice comes out hoarse. "Syd, you didn't have to get me anything."

"Open it!"

I set the tissue paper back and pull out a mug that says Handsome Devil. There's little devil horns above the words.

"Do you like it?" she asks.

I curl my hand around the back of her neck, pulling her close, and kiss her. I rest my forehead against hers. "I love it." *And I think I love you.*

She cups my face in both hands. "Good. Now feed me."

"You realize what this means?"

"What?" she asks, a smile playing over her lips.

"No more casual sex. We can only have the serious kind now."

She beams, stroking my beard. "Is that right?"

I hold up my present. "I thought the mug made that clear. You give a guy a mug, you might as well say I'm off the market. He's the one."

She laughs, and then her eyes soften. "Wyatt."

We're official.

After the mug revelation, I immediately start telling everyone Sydney's in love with me—the waiter at the Mexican-Jewish restaurant, the parking garage attendant in the city, and then the next day, my sister and Sydney's bartender and waitstaff. I say it in front of her because it makes her blush, which is funny, but I'm really just waiting for her to agree before I admit it.

Things are moving fast with Sydney, but I can't seem to help myself. It's like when you've been hacking away at a program that keeps crashing, and then suddenly it works. Magic. That's how it is with Sydney. We click on every level.

It's now the first Saturday of February, and she hasn't said a word about how she's going to make this month's payment toward her debt. I stop by her restaurant regularly. She gets a good crowd at the bar on the weekends, and her ladies' night and trivia night have followers, but it's not enough. I don't want her to be stressed month after month, barely scraping by. I give generously to those I love, even if I haven't said it in so many words. In any case, I'm stepping in to solve the problem. This isn't business. It's way past that. This is a gift to the woman I'm crazy about.

I open the glass door of Robinson Martial Arts Academy in an old white clapboard house and head upstairs to the main door. It's nearly noon on a Saturday, and I'm hoping to catch Sydney's older brother Drew on his lunch break. He's the one who inherited The Horseman Inn and wanted to sell. Sydney told me her brothers Drew and Caleb always work here together on Saturday, their busiest day. Drew owns the dojo. Caleb works there when he's not going to the city for modeling gigs. She shares a lot about her brothers. They're close, which I like, because my family is too. When you lose a parent young, it brings the siblings closer together.

There's a row of black plastic chairs in a small waiting area filled mostly with dads. A class of twenty kids, boys and girls around ten years old, are moving through a series of movements while Drew and Caleb watch at the head of the class. I've seen all of her brothers around The Horseman Inn at one point or another. Usually to watch a game and hang at the bar, but Eli also plays acoustic guitar there sometimes. The kids are on a raised blue platform that reminds me of what gymnasts use for flooring, probably with some spring to it. White flexible ropes surround the platform, and a long length of mirror is mounted on the wall for the class to see themselves.

Drew barks out something I don't understand. *Japanese?* It

sounds like *kata* something. Caleb and the kids move into another choreographed series of movements, ending with a punch and kick. Both Drew and Caleb wear black belts around their white karate uniforms. The kids are mostly orange and purple belts and look very serious.

"Good," Drew says. "Practice that new *kata* daily."

"Yes, Sensei," the class choruses in unison.

"I'll see you next week," he says.

They bow to him before filing out of the ring in an orderly line. The kids are talking to each other, but not too loudly. I'm surprised at how well behaved they are.

Drew and Caleb follow the class off the mat. Caleb gets to me first. He's got a buzz cut and an open friendly face. "Hey, Wyatt, what're you doing here? Looking to sign up for a class?"

"No, actually, I was hoping to talk to Drew."

"Wyatt," Drew says as he steps off the mat, "what's up?"

"Just wanted to talk to you if you have a minute. In private."

He nods once. "Give me a few minutes."

I hang back while Drew and Caleb mingle with the parents and say goodbye to the kids.

"Next class doesn't start for fifteen minutes," Drew says, returning to my side. "Come back to my office."

I follow him around the corner to a small office with an old wood desk and a black mesh office chair. He indicates I should take the plastic chair opposite him. I do, suddenly unnerved by his hard expression staring at me across the desk, his brown eyes direct, his scruffy jaw tight. This is the first time we've spoken one-on-one, and he's giving off a menacing vibe. *Does he know I'm sleeping with his sister?*

I clear my throat. "I've been seeing Sydney. Has she mentioned it?"

He leans back in his chair, his expression unreadable. "No."

"Uh, okay, well, we are. So I know the restaurant isn't doing well. I have a plan to help her, and I'd like to talk to you about it because I know you inherited the place."

"I transferred the deed to her name."

"Ah." That makes this more difficult. The woman is stubborn—her only flaw—but I can work around that. I barrel on, figuring if he's on board with my plan, he can back me up. "I want to help her out. I can buy it, clearing the debt, and then I'd like to renovate and hire a new chef. Farm-to-table restaurants are popular right now, and in this area it's something we could pull off. There's enough suppliers nearby. I'd keep Sydney on as manager. I'd have a say, of course, as owner."

He remains leaning back in his chair, studying me.

"Or we could be co-owners. I'd be willing to keep her name on the deed."

The silence is unnerving. *Is the man made of ice?* I can't tell if he's about to put me in a chokehold or agree with my plan.

I continue. "She says if she misses a payment, she's facing foreclosure. I hate to see her stressed about this month after month. I can fix this."

He straightens, his dark eyes piercing. "Have you told Sydney your plan?"

"Yes, but she, uh, hasn't agreed entirely." *Or at all. And I changed the plan from a loan to an outright buy to do it up right because I'm crazy about her.*

More unnerving silence.

"I know she doesn't want to lose the place, and I want her to keep it. I have a good track record at turning failing businesses around."

"Sounds good," he says simply.

I let out a breath of relief. "Great! I'm glad you agree." I stand. "Thanks for your time."

"But you'll have to get Sydney on board," he says.

I stop in the doorway of his office. "I will."

His lips twitch. "Last I heard, you were Satan."

I grin. "She calls me Beelzebub. Cute, right? Obviously she's in love with me."

His brows lift.

I leave on that note, chuckling to myself. I like telling everyone she's in love with me. Makes me feel better about already falling for her.

~

Sydney

I finish checking on the dinner preparations in the kitchen with George, the dependable chef who used to work for my dad. He's in his late sixties now, but still as happy as a clam ruling over the kitchen with the help of two line cooks.

"Don't worry, Sydney," he says, stirring a tomato sauce. "I could do this in my sleep. Been cooking here since before you were born."

"I know, but I just have to make the rounds. Thanks, George!"

I head through the dining area, which is empty since it's only a little before five. Oh! Drew's at the bar. It's early for him. Usually he'll stop by around seven or later. I swear half the time he's just checking up on me and couldn't care less what game is on TV. He's in a blue Henley with jeans and hiking boots. His brown hair is slicked back like he just took a shower. He needs a shave too.

I walk over to him, smiling. "Don't you have a blow dryer at your place?" He's too manly for that. His three-bedroom ranch house reminds me of a military barracks—sparse, neat, done in beige and black.

"No."

"I'm going to get you one." I poke his wet hair. "You're lucky this didn't turn to ice in these freezing temperatures."

He studies me in his intense way. He doesn't miss much. "You're in a good mood."

I look away, not wanting to admit I'm now sleeping with Satan. I mean, how often did I complain about the man? Everyone knew he drove me crazy. I told my friends the deal, of course, since I've been spending all my free time with him. He's just so wonderful. I have zero complaints. He always makes sure I get off first, and just the fact that I even get off at all is way better than my last boyfriend. And that's not all! He takes me out when I have off work, and makes me meals at his place when I don't. Granted, they're simple meals in the toaster and microwave, but he's taking care of me. In my experience, most guys expect you to take care of them. It's a nice change of pace. We can talk for hours. And he's affectionate too. He's just so much more than I ever expected.

"Syd?"

"Huh?"

"I said can we talk in private?"

My good mood vanishes. Drew never wants to talk to me in private. "Sounds serious," I manage. "Is everything okay? Is it Adam? Eli? Caleb?" My heart races, thinking of something bad happening to one of my brothers.

"Nothing like that." He stands. "Why don't we sit at that corner table?"

I look over to the table in the back room, the same one that Wyatt always chooses. "Why there?"

He walks ahead of me. "Because it's private."

Does he know about me and Wyatt? Did he confront Wyatt in a misguided overprotective big-brother move? How embarrassing. I really hope it's not that.

I follow him over to the corner table and sit across from him.

"I saw Wyatt earlier," he says.

"What did you say to him?" I hold my breath, praying it wasn't too embarrassing. What if he told him to be careful with me because I had a bad breakup? Or warned him if he hurt me, he'd kick his ass? I'm dying to text Wyatt to hear his side because Drew isn't always forthcoming with all the details.

"I told him his plan was a good idea, but he had to get you on board. Syd, I think you should do it."

"What plan?"

"I'm talking about this place."

I go very still. "What did he say?"

"You don't know? He said he ran it by you."

"Why did he go to you?"

"He thought I was the owner."

I clench my jaw. "So he went behind my back to take over my restaurant?"

"He wants to save it, so let him. He says you can stay on

as manager and co-owner."

"Of course I'd be manager, and I *am* the owner. The *full* owner."

He shakes his head. "Here's the plan." Then he outlines point by point exactly what Wyatt intends to do. Didn't I tell him I wasn't willing to let him take over my place? I said I would figure it out. I still have time. It's only the first Saturday of the month. I'm trying another bank. How dare Wyatt arrange all this behind my back!

I stand. "No."

"Think about it," he says.

"I did before and now—" I look to the ceiling and rock my head side to side "—still no."

"Sit down," he orders. He's used to giving orders that are obeyed.

I glare at him.

"Please," he says through his teeth.

I drop back into my seat. "What? There's nothing more to talk about."

"Tell me why you won't take this offer. It solves everything."

"Because it's my family's legacy not his! Robinsons have owned this place for generations. I'm not going to lose it to an outsider!"

He looks over my shoulder. "Here comes your outsider, and I think he heard that."

I stand and turn to face Wyatt and Kayla standing just a few feet away.

Our waitress, Ellen, also here since my father's time, looks over at me. "Are you and Drew having dinner at that corner table, or is it okay for Wyatt to have his table?"

"It's not his table," I grind out.

Wyatt gestures toward it. "I do sit there every time I come here."

Drew walks by and jerks his chin at Wyatt. Kayla stares at Drew with wide-eyed avid curiosity, watching as he walks back to the bar.

I stop in front of Wyatt. "Hi, Kayla, you can take the table. We'll just be a minute."

Wyatt smirks. "Problem, she-devil?"

16

He's smirking, and I'm not playing right now. I point at the corner table. "This is not your table. It will never be your table. I own this place down to the last cobweb in the dark corner of the basement."

"Gross, and I know that. It was a figure of speech, asking for my table."

I lower my voice, as a family is seated in the front dining room nearby. "What the hell do you think you're doing going behind my back to talk to Drew?"

"Is this really the time and place you want to do this? You've got customers now."

"Fine. Let's go upstairs to my place."

He tugs a lock of my hair. "So soon? I haven't even had dinner yet."

I seethe. "It'll take five minutes."

"I don't know if I can get it done that quick, but I'll try my best."

I press my lips together so I don't scream at him. Wouldn't look good in front of the customers. Instead I call over to Kayla, "He'll be back in five minutes."

"Okay, I'm going to order a drink. Wyatt, I'll get you a beer."

"Just water," he says.

Because he thinks my beer sucks. He's used to high-end bars in the city where drinks start at twenty-five dollars. And who cares when you have billions to throw around and get your way doing whatever you want whenever you want?

I grab his hand and lead him through the kitchen to the rear staircase that leads upstairs.

"Hey, everyone," he says to the kitchen staff. "I'm with her. She's in love with me."

I march up the steps, not amused. "Stop telling everyone I'm in love with you. Not cool at my place of work."

He pats my ass. "Sorry about that. I'll keep it to friends and family."

"Don't say it at all!"

I unlock the door and head down the short hallway to my room. He stops in the doorway, taking in the small space. It's just a twin-size bed, nightstand, and a garment rack on wheels.

He peers down the hall. "Where's the rest of it?"

"It's just this room and a bathroom. The main room is used as storage for restaurant stuff."

He walks in and sits next to me on the bed. "Look at this girly blanket."

It's a red blanket with white flowers. *Does he have to comment on everything?*

"Okay, enough about my crappy apartment," I say. "It's temporary. Stop trying to fix my whole life."

He raises his palms. "If you want to live in a crappy apartment, that's fine by me. As long as you stay at my place regularly. Hey, maybe Kayla could stay here, and you could just shift your, uh—" he looks over at my garment rack of hanging clothes with a bunch of stuff thrown haphazardly over it "—you could just pack a suitcase."

My lips part in surprise. He wants me to move in with him?

He lifts one shoulder in a casual shrug, his eyes warm on mine. My heart thumps harder at that warm-eyed look. "Just an idea."

I have the sudden urge to kiss him. Sometimes he's just

too appealing, but then I remember I'm mad. "We need to get a few things straight."

"I agree."

"You do?"

"Absolutely, I want this problem solved quickly, as I told your brother."

I clench my teeth. "Why did you go behind my back to Drew instead of talking to me about your plans?"

"I did tell you weeks ago, that night you were trapped at my place. You weren't exactly agreeable. And haven't I mentioned several times that a farm-to-table concept could do a lot for your place?"

"Yes, and I don't disagree with that, but it's not a priority right now."

"And your chef is a family friend who can't learn a whole new style of cooking."

"I'm sure he could learn if he wanted to…" *Probably not.* "The point is, it would be an insult to ask him. And he's been here since my dad took over the restaurant years and years ago."

"So you just let the place die because of attachment to what it was. You're in charge now. You can bring it into a new phase of success."

I open my mouth and close it. Somehow he seems to be on my side now, talking about me being in charge. "Exactly, I'm the owner."

"And I could be co-owner. You need me. This isn't a loan either. The debt disappears. I want you to be happy."

I take a deep breath. He means well, I can see that, but the way he went about it rubs me wrong.

He shifts toward me. "Drew knew this restaurant isn't working, which is why he wanted to sell in the first place. You jumped in, but it's still a mess through no fault of your own. Let me fix it. You can still be manager if you want."

At my silence, he continues. "We'd be more of a partnership. And we'll add to the employee handbook that fraternization is encouraged among employees."

"There is no employee handbook."

"Then I'll make one and be sure to put it right there in black and white that partners can have wild monkey sex whenever the urge strikes."

I fight back a smile. He's funny, but now is not the time. "You can't have a piece of the place that's been in my family for generations. No outsiders. It's a Robinson business."

"I'm more of an *insider* now," he says with a smirk. He's making a sex joke.

I leap off the bed. "This is serious!"

He stands and cradles my jaw with one large hand, gazing into my eyes. "Syd, this is who I am. I'm a fixer. That's how I got Snowball. And, yes, I love my cute little dog with her fluffy hair. There, I said it. Same deal with my sisters. I love them, and I fix whatever's broken."

My brain connects the dots. He fixes things for those he loves, me included. I want to protest I don't need any help, but my throat's clogged with emotion over what he's really saying. He's been telling everyone I'm in love with him because *he's* the one in love with *me*. After my ex fell out of love with me, I spent way too long wondering what was wrong with me that made him stop loving me. Maybe it wasn't a problem with me after all. And the truth is, I'm in love with Wyatt, and I've been too chicken to say it.

"Syd?"

"You don't love me. It's too soon." *Please say you do.*

He kisses me. "Okay."

I can tell he's placating me, and that makes me all warm and gooey inside because he secretly loves me. My stomach does a topsy-turvy flip. "Don't say things you don't mean."

"Never, unless you ask me if your ass looks fat in those jeans. That answer will always be no. Been there, got the door slammed on my own ass as I was kicked out."

I meet his whiskey eyes sparkling with good humor. "You can't fix all my problems. I'm handling it."

"How?"

"It's my problem, okay? I don't want you involved. I'm not with you for your money, and I'm not budging on owner-ship of my place. You hear me?"

"I feel you." He cups my ass and presses me firmly against me. "You feel me?"

I smile reluctantly. "Swear you won't interfere in my business unless I ask you to."

His eyes are intent on mine. "Ask me."

"No."

"So damn stubborn."

He leans in for a kiss, and I put a hand on his chest. "Wyatt."

"Okay, okay. I won't interfere."

And then he's kissing me again, and I can't help it. I throw my arms around him and kiss him back.

~

By noon on Monday, I have my answer from the bank—no. It's time for me to go to Harper, even though it pains me to do so. Wyatt's gesture is well-meaning, but it comes with strings I simply can't accept.

I work up a loan agreement for Harper and, because I'm really anxious, a letter that states exactly the business terms that she can expect from me, including regular updates on the restaurant's financial statements and paying it back more quickly if things improve. We've been friends forever, and I want to be clear I'm not taking advantage of her fame. She's worked hard for it and doesn't deserve the users that are drawn to her sweet generous nature. I still feel queasy about it. She's got a lot on her plate right now with her upcoming wedding, baby, and aging grandmother, so if she can't give me the full amount, that's okay. It'll buy me some time to build my customer base.

I'm at home for my day off. I stand, looking out the window at the sparse tree line and a few homes. With the leaves gone, I can see all the way to Lake Summerdale. It's quiet out there, snow still covering everything. The lake has a thin sheet of ice on it. If the ice gets thick enough, the town rec department will put a green flag out that it's safe for ice skating. Today it's just the drab dead of winter out there. Yet whenever I'm with Wyatt, it feels like spring is just around the corner. A bubbly jubilant feeling. *Love.*

I shake my head and pull my phone out of my hoodie pocket. Lately I'm so dreamy, my mind constantly drifting to Wyatt. Yesterday at his place, we all made s'mores in the fireplace and laughed and talked so much. I grilled Kayla on Wyatt stories growing up. She told me he used to spend forever styling his hair before school, making his sisters crazy, who needed to do their hair too. Two bathrooms for the four of them. Lots of screaming. And she claimed he'd come out looking exactly as he had going in. He said that was the style back then. Ha!

My phone chimes in my hand. Daydreaming again. It's a text from Wyatt: *Kayla's going home for a visit. Crew leaves at five. You know what that means.*

I smile.

Wyatt: *Naked Sydney on the island.*

He's always teasing about wanting me in the kitchen. I may get a little handsy watching him prepare meals for me.

I text back. *How about naked Wyatt on the island?*

That works too. What time will you be here? I need to make sure I have enough microwave burritos.

Mexican again?

Mexican always. Time? I need to prepare.

I want to ask him what he's preparing, but then I think better of it. He probably wants to surprise me.

Me: *What time do you want me there?*

Wyatt: *Now.*

My hand goes to my heart, warmth flooding me. I love that he doesn't play games, pretending he's not too interested in me. He loves me. I felt it from almost the beginning with the warmth in his eyes, and it's only grown stronger day by day.

Me: *I can be there in an hour.*

Wyatt: *Snowball is annoyed she has to wait so long, but I'll let her know it's just because you want to wash your hair, shave your legs, all that good stuff in anticipation of an extended naked time under the kitchen lights.*

Little does he know I already did all that.

Me: *Could you at least pretend you don't know all that girl stuff?*

Wyatt: *Blame my sisters. I know all. (Involuntarily.)*

Me: *See you soon.*

Wyatt: *Not soon enough. That's Snowball. Always so eager to see you.*

I stare at my phone, smiling. *Oh, Wyatt.*

I shake my head, realizing I've been standing here smiling at my phone for I don't know how long. I call Harper, and thankfully she answers.

"Hi, Harp. It's Sydney."

"Is everything okay? Your voice sounds a little weird."

"Yes, fine. I'm good." *Happy.* It's weird to feel so happy when I'm making the call I've been dreading. "The restaurant isn't doing well though. I hate to ask, but I've missed three payments, and if—"

"Not another word. Consider it done. I'm happy to send payment for the full amount."

"Are you sure? It's two hundred thousand. I know you've got your wedding and the baby and—"

"It's fine. I have a nice little nest egg. You know I've never led an extravagant lifestyle."

My eyes water. "Thank you. I'll pay you back. I worked up the paperwork and a letter outlining all the terms. I never want money to come between us, okay? This will all be very businesslike, and I'll keep you in the loop at all times."

"Of course. I know you're good for it."

"I wouldn't ask if it wasn't such a dire situation. I never want you to think I'm taking advantage of you being famous. I know you've had users in your life who didn't treat you—"

"Seriously? Syd, all this time I thought you just didn't want to mix business with friendship. You actually thought I'd feel used by you? You've been my fiercest, most vocal supporter through every up and down my entire life."

I swallow over the lump of emotion lodged in my throat. "Are you saying I'm a loudmouth?"

"Yes! When we both tried out for drama club shows and I

got the lead every time, even though you were also fantastic and way funnier, you told everyone to watch, that one day I'd be a star."

"You are a star."

"You think I could've made it where I am today without your unwavering confidence in me?"

I shake my head. "That was all your talent. You didn't need me."

"The hell I didn't. I knew you always had my back. You, Jenna, Audrey, you're like sisters to me." Her voice cracks.

A tear leaks out of my eye. "Oh, crap. Now you're making me cry."

She laughs a little. "Sorry, I'm hormonal from the pregnancy. Everything makes me cry. I don't want you to spend another moment worrying about this. Nothing will ever come between me and my honorary sisters. We're sisters for life."

Sisters for life. I let out a choking sob, tears streaming down my face, and I am *not* a crier. It's just that Harper is an only child, and I only had brothers. "Dammit. Look what you made me do with all this sister business." I grab a tissue and wipe my tears while the two of us sit on the phone sniffling to each other.

"Oh, Syd. If I'd known this was what you were so worried about, I would've made you cry earlier."

"Ha-ha."

"Seriously, though, between me and Garrett, we're fine. We can spare it. I'll have my accountant transfer the money to your account today. Tell me all your info, and I'll pass it on to her."

"Okay, and I'll email you the paperwork I came up with. Hold on." I dig my papers out from the nightstand drawer. She goes over my bank info with me twice, and then we talk a bit about her upcoming wedding on Saturday, Valentine's Day. I'm going to be a bridesmaid. Josie Abbott is her matron of honor. I can't wait to meet her. She's a famous actress and super funny.

"Thanks again, Harp. Anything you need, any time, you call. I could hold your hand in the delivery room or babysit or check on General Joan weekly. Whatever you want." The General is her elderly grandmother.

"I'd like daily General Joan checks for the next year."

I swallow hard. "Really?" Her grandmother is tough as nails and would not be so fun to visit daily. She'd probably order me to clean out her basement while supervising with her eagle eye, barking out commands. The woman really missed her calling in the military.

She laughs. "Kidding. You don't owe me anything. I just want you to be happy."

"I am. Actually, things are going really well with Wyatt."

"I'm not at all surprised."

"Don't you remember I used to call him Satan? He made me so mad." I can't put much heat into my voice feeling the way I do now, all warm and affectionate.

"Puh-lease. The sparks between you two were about to set the place on fire. I told you he's a good guy."

"Yeah, he is."

"Aww, you really like him, don't you?"

I do a little wiggle in place. "I'm in love with him, and vice versa."

"I'm so happy for you! Next time you get time off, you guys should come into the city to visit us. We'll be at my place for a couple more months before we move into our new place in Brooklyn. We're having some renovations done. Garrett and his brothers took it on since January's their slow time."

"I'll mention it. Sounds good. Thanks again."

"You're quite welcome. Talk soon, sistah. Bye."

I flop back on my bed, weak with relief. Problem solved. And I didn't need Wyatt for any of it.

17

A short while later, I go to Wyatt's place. I ring the bell at his front door, and he answers, Snowball tucked under one arm. He's wearing a light blue button-down shirt with the top two buttons undone, displaying golden manly chest, with dark gray trousers and leather shoes. He looks simultaneously sexy and nurturing the way he holds Snowball. My ovaries do a little dance. This man is father material. We're not there yet, but I like the potential. Suddenly I just want to throw my arms around him. I resist, embarrassed by jumping so far ahead in my mind. "Hi."

He jerks his head. "Quick, get in here. I don't want dinner to burn."

"You're cooking?"

"Yup." He kisses me. "Glad you're here. Let's go." He sets Snowball down, who trots after him to the kitchen.

I take off my jacket and hang it on a hook in the foyer. I take a moment to check my purple cashmere sweater for lint. It was a birthday gift from my dad two years ago. Always so generous, even when he shouldn't have been. I'm in jeans and my dressy high-heeled ankle boots. I didn't know he was cooking a special dinner, but I always take the time to look nice before I come over.

I go to the kitchen just as Wyatt's draining a colander into the sink. It smells like steak in here. I spot two rib eye steaks, fully cooked, resting on top of the stove. "This looks great." I'm so surprised he's cooking, based on what we've been eating, mostly frozen microwavable food. "You actually like cooking?"

"Sometimes," he says, reading something on his phone.

I peek over his shoulder. He's got a mashed potato recipe on his phone. "Usually just some milk, butter, salt, and pepper."

He looks at me over his shoulder. "Excuse me, I can't impress you if you help. Take a seat at the island."

I sit and watch as he prepares the potatoes. Once that's done, he pulls a plastic bag of green beans from the refrigerator and microwaves them. "I got the kind you can cook in the bag."

I smile. "This is really nice."

He goes to a cabinet and takes out two crystal wineglasses. "I got your favorite merlot."

"I told you my favorite merlot?"

"You talk constantly in bed. I listen."

My cheeks heat. "I do not talk constantly."

He smiles. "You share quite a bit post orgasm. There's a balance—too many orgasms and you fall asleep. Too little and you're all over me for hours." He widens his eyes. "Exhausting. Just right, and you're chatting away."

I can't decide if I'm embarrassed that he tracks me like this or just happy he's so good at making me feel good. "No such thing as too many orgasms."

He arches a brow. "Should we test it?"

A rush of desire goes through me. "Stop. Get back to dinner."

"It could be a fun experiment." He pulls the green beans from the microwave and cuts the top open, dropping it on the counter. "We never made it to six."

I shiver at the thought.

A short while later, we're settled across from each other at the kitchen table with our dinner of steak, mashed potatoes, and green beans. It's simple but really good. We both have a glass of wine.

"So is this your go-to seduction meal for your dates?" I ask.

"No, what? Why would you say that? This is a complete original." He nods.

"I'm going to pretend you just made it for me so it's special." I cut off another piece of steak. "Besides, it's awesome. I was expecting microwave burritos. Thanks for cooking."

"You're welcome. In the morning I'm going to make you French toast."

"Oh my God, I love French toast." I take a sip of merlot with hints of plum and dark cherry. "This wine is amazing. What kind is it?"

He goes back to the counter, where he left the bottle, and brings it over. It's a California wine I've never heard of. It must've been expensive. "I never have this quality of wine. I'm strictly on the under-twenty-dollar wine budget."

"Stick with me," he says. "I've got excellent taste."

And money. I keep that to myself. Instead I smile and take another sip. I can't enjoy what his money can buy and feel like it's too much at the same time. I don't want him because of his money, which is another reason I don't want to let him get involved in my debt problem. At least that's taken care of. Harper told me to confirm the money's in my account in the morning, and then I'll immediately send payment out to clear my debt once and for all.

I take a forkful of mashed potatoes. "Harper says we should visit her and Garrett in the city."

He sets his fork down with a clatter. "Oh really? Sounds like a very couple thing to do."

I flush hot, mortified I overstepped. "I didn't mean to assume that you and I are…" *Wait a minute, the man implied very clearly he loves me.* "Ha-ha."

He smirks. "Had you for a minute there." He picks up his fork and goes back to his steak.

I glance at him. "Some guys are weird about that stuff."

"You're mine. That's all I need to know."

I suck in air. "I'm yours?"

"Yeah." He chews and spares me a glance. "You can call it whatever you want, boyfriend-girlfriend, couple, relationship. All the same to me. I know you're mine."

I give him side-eye. "That sounds a little too possessive to me."

"Not at all. I'm a giver. See? I cooked you dinner; later I'll fuck your brains out. Give, give, give. Possessive would be holding you tight to me. I'm giving to you with my hands wide open." He cocks his head. "Or is that my heart?"

A bubble of pure happiness rises in me, making me feel light and buoyant. What guy talks about opening his heart? No guy, that's who. I walk around to his side of the table and hug him.

"Careful," he says. "I'm holding a steak knife here."

I release him, and he stands, sets the knife down, and kisses me tenderly.

He frames my face with both hands. "I love you."

My eyes get hot. He implied he did several times, he showed it in his actions, but still the words get to me deep down. A surge of affection overwhelms me, making my heart feel full to bursting. "I love you too." I kiss him and pull away, but I can't resist those warm whiskey eyes on mine, so I kiss him again. And again.

He grins. "I know you want me, but finish your dinner. I put a lot of planning into this. Finest cut of meat. Hours of internet research for the best recipes. This was a step up from my usual seduction meal. Only the best for you."

My heart squeezes. *Wait, hours of research for mashed potatoes and microwave-in-the-bag green beans. Ha!*

I guess he researched the heck out of steak recipes.

I smile and go back to my seat. "You know, if I'm yours, then that means you're mine."

He lifts his brows. "Fact. I knew we had to be exclusive from the start. I mean, how could I possibly have any stamina left for anyone else the way you attack me every night?"

I laugh. "Damn right."

He gives me his warm smile, his eyes gazing into mine. "Damn good."

Wyatt

It's awesome to have Sydney all to myself here. I don't begrudge my sister's presence, but I'm definitely more relaxed just me and Syd. She's more relaxed too. After dinner, things got dirty on top of the island. And later in my bed. In the shower this morning too, but that was her pleasuring me. I can't remember ever feeling this good.

Now I'm making her my signature French toast. The secret is vanilla extract. She's sitting at the kitchen island, sipping coffee, checking her phone. I told her it's about time she started sexting me, so hopefully she's getting right on that. I smile to myself.

She gasps. "Oh my God."

"What?"

She stares at her phone, eyes wide, and then looks at me. "There has to be a mistake. I have to call her." She rushes from the room.

Strange. Call who? What kind of mistake? I hope it wasn't anything to do with her debt problem. After breakfast, I was going to try to convince her to accept my help and partner with me. I want to take the burden off her shoulders.

I finish up the French toast, get out the syrup, and set a couple of plates on the island for us. Almost forgot the sausage. I get several links from the freezer and microwave that too.

I settle at the island a few minutes later, and she returns, her eyes glassy. Now I'm really getting worried.

I close the distance and wrap my arms around her. "What happened?"

"Harper added another hundred thousand onto my loan. She said she wanted to give me some breathing room while I get the restaurant back on its feet." She stares at my chest.

"It's so generous. I know I should be happy, but it's going to take *forever* to pay her back."

I drop my arms from her, my gut tight. She shut me out, going to Harper instead of me. She doesn't trust in my abilities. Maybe I'm new to the restaurant business, but I have a lot of great ideas. I'm the fixer. I offered to help her out, free and clear, no loan. That's a way better deal than owing money to Harper. Obviously, Sydney doesn't want me as her partner. She says she loves me, but she still keeps me at a distance. The outsider.

My chest aches. Hell, I thought we were building something here.

I keep my voice calm. "Why wouldn't you take my money but you'll take hers?"

"I don't want to owe you anything."

I work for patience. "I said you didn't have to pay me back. Just include me in saving the business."

She returns to her seat at the island. "I'm not one of your sisters you need to rescue. Let's not fight. Breakfast smells wonderful." She sits in front of it and cuts off a piece of French toast, popping it in her mouth.

I'm too mad to eat. "Why won't you let me fix this?" She's pushing me away. Not only that, she kept me in the dark about Harper fixing her problem. It occurs to me I kept her in the dark when I went to Drew, but it's not like I didn't mention how to fix her restaurant before that. And I thought he was the owner at the time. I had a legitimate reason to go to him. She had no reason to go to Harper. She has me.

I stare at her. "You won't accept my help doing what I do best. I turn businesses around. I take care of people. In this case, my two strengths are united—taking care of you and saving your business, yet you shut me out."

"Wyatt," she says gently, "it's not personal. Seriously."

Of course it's personal. And I'm not letting her owe another huge debt. That's no way to live.

I love her deeply. And, after all her struggles, I'm fixing this once and for all.

As soon as Sydney leaves my place for work that morning, I call Harper.

Harper answers the phone cheerfully. "Hi, Wyatt. Sydney tells me things are great between you. I'm thrilled to hear it."

"Not quite."

"Oh no. Did you guys break up?"

"No, nothing like that. She's in love with me, but she's too damn stubborn to accept my help."

"Aww."

"I want to pay off her loan to you. She's stubborn, as you know, and keeps insisting she doesn't want me mixed up in this, but I am, so give me your info, and I'll clear her debt to you."

"I don't know. Maybe you two should talk about it first?"

"We did talk. Look, it's serious with us, so just consider it an engagement gift for her in the future."

"An engagement gift before the engagement?"

"I'll let her know after she says yes. Better than jewelry for her, don't you think?"

"That's so romantic. You're looking out for her."

"Yes! Thank you. That's what I keep telling her, but she's Miss Independent."

"This is so sweet. You guys fell fast."

"It's been a month, and we were working up to it for a while before that. She just didn't see my charm at first."

She laughs. "Okay. I'll text you my accountant's number, and you can call her to work out the details."

"Thanks. Very much appreciated."

18

———

Sydney

It's Thursday, and I'm feeling awesome. Trivia night and Thursday Night Wine Club, aka ladies' night, are growing in popularity, and my debt is gone. The Horseman Inn is free and clear. I can make payroll, invest in marketing, even consider some renovations. The kitchen badly needs upgrades.

I'm going to Wyatt's place after work tonight, like usual. We're essentially living together. With Kayla too. She decided to stay and work on her thesis there. She finds Summerdale charming and enjoys all the land surrounding Wyatt's place. She even bought snowshoes so she could tromp around the property. She'll take Snowball on walks that way, where the snow isn't too deep.

It's around midnight when I get to Wyatt's place. He's expecting me and meets me at the door with a bouquet of red roses in one hand, Snowball tucked under his arm. She keeps sniffing the roses.

"For you," he says warmly.

"Wow." I take the roses and kiss him. "Thank you."

He puts Snowball down and helps me off with my coat, hanging it on the hook. Snowball trots back toward the sofa room, where Kayla sleeps. Wyatt keeps her doggie bed there now. Kayla takes Snowball out in the morning.

"Such a gentleman tonight," I tease. "Is Kayla up?"

"She's sleeping. Working on her thesis puts her to sleep. It would put anyone to sleep. You want something to drink or eat?"

I shake my head.

"Upstairs?"

I smile. "Yeah." He still only has the one bedroom set up.

He cups my jaw and kisses me tenderly. His fingers stroke down my throat. "Give me a few minutes to prepare."

"Okay. Can I freshen up in the bathroom, or is that where you're, uh, preparing?" I have no idea what he's up to. Another romantic gift upstairs? Preparing his body in some way? Not that it needs it. He's gorgeous.

"Let me check on one thing." He rushes upstairs. A moment later, he says, "Okay, come on up."

I follow him, intrigued. His bedroom door is closed. Maybe he got his furniture out of storage and wants to surprise me, though I thought he'd put that in the master bedroom. But no, they're renovating the master bedroom to add an en suite bathroom and walk-in closet by adjoining the room next door.

He waves me past the bedroom, a smile tugging at his lips. "Move along. Nothing to see here."

I smile. "Okay, if you say so." I'm dying to peek but continue on to the bathroom to get ready for bed. I have an extra set of toiletries here now for convenience. Once I'm ready, I debate walking out in just my bra and panties—they are my nice red satin ones that push up my ample breasts—but I refrain. If he has a gift for me, that will distract him too much, and I won't get it until I'm too spent to open my eyes. The way he wrings every last drop of pleasure from my body is phenomenal. Hands down, the best lover I've ever had. Or is it mouth down? He's generous in that department too.

I step out of the bathroom, still wearing my black uniform T-shirt, black skinny jeans, and cozy sheepskin boots. When I get to the bedroom door, it's still closed.

I knock. "Can I come in now?"

Wyatt opens the door and gestures for me to come in. My breath catches. He strung white twinkle lights along the ceiling and sprinkled red rose petals on the bed in the shape of an arrow.

I laugh. "Am I supposed to follow the arrow and climb into bed?"

"Get a little closer and see."

I turn back to him, smiling. "It's so romantic."

"That's me." He rocks his head side to side. "With you anyway."

I follow the rose petal arrow to the pillow. There's a small robin's egg blue box tied with a white ribbon. *A Tiffany box.* My heart races. "Wyatt?" I croak.

He comes up behind me, wrapping his arms around me. His voice is husky. "Open it."

"That looks expensive."

"It's yours. Go ahead and open it."

I stare at it. "You didn't have to get me an expensive present." I turn in his arms. "I'm not about money. That's not why I'm with you."

He frames my face with his hands. "I know. I want you to have it."

I swallow hard. *Is this what I think it is?* Maybe it's just earrings. Oh God. I turn back to the gift, unable to move. I need to know how I'll answer. I love him; he loves me.

"You're going to make me do this, aren't you?" He snags the gift, tugging the ribbon off. He takes the smaller box out and goes down on one knee. "Will you marry me?"

I slap a hand over my mouth.

He looks down at the box. "Forgot to open it. This is my first proposal." He opens the box to a huge round solitaire diamond on a platinum band. At least I think it's platinum. The light is dim from the twinkling lights.

I rush to the light switch and turn it on, staring at Wyatt on one knee, an engagement ring in hand. Yup, that's definitely a multi-carat diamond set on platinum. I grip my trembling hands together.

"Syd?" he prompts. "Are you going to answer me?"

"I need to think about it," I blurt.

He snaps the box closed and stands. "Too soon?"

"It feels quick. I'm just not sure. We haven't talked about it before." I can't seem to catch my breath. I walk over to the bed and sit down.

He shoves the box in his pocket and sits next to me. "Let's talk about it now. We love each other. I'm going to marry you."

"You're just telling me this." I laugh, but it comes out shaky.

"Well, I asked, and you didn't answer. So yes. I'm going to marry you. You're going to run The Horseman Inn, live with me here, and one day our kids will inherit the restaurant."

"Our kids," I echo, my head spinning. I have never in my life had a guy look to the future with me with such absolute certainty. "Is it too fast?"

"Sometimes it happens that way." He takes my hand in his. "Your hand is so clammy. I really did surprise you, didn't I? I'm new at this whole proposal thing. We're both experienced enough to recognize when it's right, and this is right."

I lean against his warmth, wrapping my arms around his middle. He puts his arm around my shoulder. "What if you regret asking? Wouldn't a broken engagement suck?"

"That won't happen."

I laugh a little. "I don't know how you can be so confident."

"Because you're crazy about me. Even Kayla commented on the hearts in your eyes." That's what I always say about Harper, so I know he's teasing.

I poke him in the ribs. "You have hearts in your eyes."

"Guilty."

I sigh. "I want to say yes, but I'm scared. What if you stop loving me?"

"I told you people only say that when there's someone else." He meets my eyes. "There's never going to be anyone else for me but you."

I straighten, searching his expression. He's absolutely sincere.

"I already got you an engagement gift too," he says.

"Another one? Besides the gazillion-carat diamond ring from Tiffany's?"

He nods, smiling.

"What is it?

He smirks. "You have to be officially engaged to me to get it."

"Is this a bribe?"

He nuzzles into my neck, kissing his way up to my ear. "Come on, Sydney, you know you want to say yes."

"Okay, yes! Yes!"

He crushes me in a hug. "You won't regret it. I swear I'll make you happy."

Tears sting my eyes; overwhelmed by all I'm feeling. It's like Christmas and my birthday all at the same time—such a great gift, our love, a future together. "Now you're making me cry."

He cradles my jaw and kisses me tenderly. "I'm so happy."

I laugh through my tears. "Me too. Put the ring on me."

He stands, retrieving the box and pulling the ring out. Then he takes my hand, brushes a kiss over the knuckles, and slides the ring on.

"It's so sparkly," I say, holding it up to the light and angling it back and forth.

"So are you."

I hear the rustle of clothes, look up, and see he's stripped naked.

"You don't waste time," I tease.

"Nope." He reaches for the hem of my T-shirt and pulls it over my head. "I go for what I want without hesitation."

"Fearless."

He pauses, stroking a finger over my breast. "I wouldn't say fearless. I had a few minutes there where I thought you were going to run screaming from my house, never to return. Scary stuff."

"Oh, Wyatt."

He sends my bra flying, and then he pulls me up off the bed, enveloping me in a warm hug. I lift my head, our lips meeting once again, his fingers stroking down my spine in a tingly path.

I break the kiss. "I can't believe we're engaged. I should tell people."

"It's after midnight." He huffs. "Clearly I'm not doing this seduction stuff right." He tackles me to the bed, and I shriek.

And then we're kissing again, but this time he's demanding, kissing me roughly. I ignite, eager to join with him, my hands all over him, stroking, scratching, pulling him closer. My lover, my fiancé.

He raises himself up just long enough to strip me naked, rolls a condom on, and returns to me, taking me in one hard thrust. I wrap my legs high around his waist, my hips arching up, taking him deep. It's a wild primal ride, our bodies slapping together, our breaths harsh.

His head drops by my ear, a sexy rumble of dirty talk. The intensity skyrockets, and then I'm gone. The breath whooshes from my lungs in a cry of ecstasy. He shudders and lets go, pumping into me and then stilling with a long groan.

I stroke his sweat-dampened hair. "I guess I can call you fiancé now."

He grunts. He's not much of a talker afterward.

I sigh happily. "I've never been a fiancée before."

He lifts his head. "I guess I should've asked before I locked it in, but did you want kids?"

"Yeah, I do."

"Me too. Okay, good. We'll work everything else out."

He rolls off me, and then he reaches over and holds my hand.

I smile so big my cheeks hurt. I can't remember ever feeling so loved, so content, so utterly satisfied.

The next morning after a rousing wake-up call from my sexy fiancé, followed by a shared shower, I step out of the steamy stall and wrap a towel around myself. Wyatt swats my ass on the way to get his towel just behind me.

I suddenly remember he had an engagement gift for me. I hope it's not too extravagant. I should get him something too. But what could I give him that he couldn't easily buy himself?

He combs his hair and turns to me. "You're awfully quiet. After making my ears bleed this morning with your screams and all that talking. "'Yes! Right there! Harder, Wyatt!'" He smirks. "Lose your voice?"

I somehow find myself blushing. I'm not used to bedroom stuff being talked about outside the bedroom.

He strokes my cheek. "You're blushing? After everything we did to each other?"

I push his hand away. "No!"

He chuckles. "Yes."

"I was just remembering you said you had an engagement present for me."

He looks in the mirror. "You think I need to trim my beard? Or maybe I should shave it."

"I like it. We're officially engaged now."

"Yup. Got the ring to prove it." He walks out of the bathroom.

I finish getting ready. He's got a double sink with a long counter with lots of drawers and cabinets. It occurs to me he was dodging the question about my present. Did he change his mind about giving it to me?

I follow him back to his room, where he's getting dressed. I pause to watch his back muscles flex as he pulls a long-sleeved rust-colored shirt on. So sexy. I have some clothes tucked in his duffel bag, he washes them for me regularly, so I slip them on. Just a simple black sweater and jeans.

He finishes getting dressed and turns to face me. "Breakfast?"

"Sure." I braid my wet hair to keep it out of my face. "Did you change your mind about giving me the engagement present? That's okay. The ring is plenty."

"No, I didn't change my mind. It's a done deal."

"Oh. I'm going to get you something too."

He snags my belt buckle and pulls me close. "You don't have to do that."

I smile. "When do I get my present?"

He gets serious. "It's not something you unwrap, but it's a gift from the heart. Understand that."

My heart squeezes, my smile huge. "Okay, what?"

"I paid off your loan to Harper."

I blink a few times, my gut doing a slow roll. "You what?"

"She thought it was a romantic engagement gift. That's how I want you to think of it." He studies my expression. "I can see you're getting worked up—"

I pull away. "Wyatt." I take a deep calming breath. "You swore you wouldn't interfere in my business unless I asked you to."

"It's not interfering. I'm helping."

"And I'm happy you want to help, but I'm still upset. You don't trust me to handle things on my own."

"You don't trust me to help."

"I don't want your help!" I exhale sharply. "Sorry. I'm just frustrated. This is the second time you went behind my back to take care of things you had no business taking care of."

He scrubs a hand over his face. "Sydney, we're getting married. Everything to do with you *is* my business."

My stomach drops. "Is that why you proposed? So you could play this off as an engagement gift?"

"No!" He looks away. "Not entirely."

"I can't believe you!"

"Look, I don't need to buy a failing restaurant. I'm doing this for you. I take care of those I love."

"I appreciate the sentiment, but do you get why I'm angry? You swore you wouldn't interfere unless I asked. I didn't ask because I'm handling it."

He lifts his palms. "What do you want from me?"

"I want you to stop being the white knight! Women don't always need to be rescued."

He scowls. "It's not a character flaw to want to help. And

you need to learn to accept help too, instead of being so stubbornly independent all the time."

"And *you* need to learn that not every problem requires you to solve it. I'm perfectly capable." I gesture, dangling my fingers high in the air. "You can't always be the puppet master in the background directing everything."

"So now I'm a puppet master? I don't make anyone do anything. There's a problem, and I fix it. That's all."

I grit my teeth. "I won't let you steamroll me. You have to respect what I decide. I told you that I handled it, and I did. Now what, you're an investor in my business and you get a say in it?"

"Why shouldn't I? I know business. I could run that side, and you can manage the place."

I shake my head, all my earlier happiness draining from me. I pull my engagement ring off. "I convinced myself this was romantic when it was all part of an orchestrated plan."

He stares at the ring, his jaw tight. "Don't."

I leave the ring on his bed. "I can't be with someone who doesn't respect me."

"I do respect you. Of course I do! But you're not perfect. You're stubborn to the point that it makes things impossibly difficult. For no good reason!" He frowns. "Why won't you let me fix this?"

My eyes sting with unshed tears. "You're not perfect either. Always the leader, always the boss, directing everything." My throat closes, tight with emotion. "Well, you can't direct me."

"Impossible woman," he mutters, shaking his head.

I grab my purse and head out the door.

I keep going, rushing through the living room, everything blurring through my tears. I grab my coat and step outside just as Kayla's returning with Snowball from their walk.

She smiles, her brown eyes sparkling. "Did you say yes?"

I shake my head and dodge past her to the safety of my car.

It's not until I'm home that I completely break down. I make it to my bed and collapse, coat, boots, and all, curling up on my side. From engaged to completely over in less than twenty-four hours. He's the impossible one. He went behind my back. Twice! I punch the pillow. He can't just take over and do what he thinks is best for me and tell me later. It hurts doubly that he disguised it all in a romantic proposal. He should've talked to me about all this.

I can't be with someone who wants to run my life just like he runs his businesses and everyone else's business who comes to him with a sob story. Or his sisters with their sob stories. Well, I am not a sob story!

I sob into my pillow. At least I wasn't until him.

19

––––––––––

Sydney

This is just perfect. I toss back a glass of expensive chardonnay and order another. It's open bar at Harper and Garrett's wedding reception. Great timing to have a wrenching breakup the day before a romantic Valentine's Day wedding. It's painful to watch someone else get married while pretending I'm just fine being single. Even worse, Wyatt's here, since he's friends with Harper and Garrett. And it's not easy to avoid him at this intimate celebration for fifty guests on the third floor of a small cooking school in Manhattan. Which is why I'm now glued to the bar. *Su-u-uck.*

Jenna and Audrey are protectively standing on either side of me. We're in matching cap-sleeve emerald green bridesmaid dresses. I gave them the briefest of explanations on Wyatt—madly in love, went behind my back twice, broke up —on our limo ride into the city. Harper sent it for us bridesmaids. We made plans for next Monday to have a real breakup recovery session at Jenna's place. With the wedding, I didn't want to get into all the nitty-gritty. It's Harper's special day, and I need to be cheerful for her. I'm really trying.

A slow song starts, the sappy lyrics making my jaw clench.

Both of my friends turn toward the small dance floor longingly.

"Wyatt's staring at you," Audrey whispers.

"No Wyatt updates, please," I say, tossing back a healthy swallow of wine. This is my second glass. And two glasses of champagne in the limo. Plus one from a passing waiter when we arrived at the reception. Two plus one plus two. I plan to stay right here until the bitter end.

A tall blond guy in his twenties with a crew cut and massive shoulders approaches Jenna, asking her to dance. Probably one of Garrett's friends.

She turns to me. "Do you mind? Are you going to be okay?"

I shoo her away. "I'm just fine here with my bartender friend." The bartender is helping someone else down at the other end of the bar, but I wave to her anyway as though we're pals.

Two more guys approach—dark hair, smiling types. I assume Garrett's friends. Harper mostly has women friends. They ask me and Audrey to dance. The biggest guy, nearly seven feet, wants Audrey. I don't know why big guys always want the petite women. Some kind of alpha-male complex.

She smiles and takes his hand, going out to the dance floor.

I shake my head at my guy still waiting for an answer. "I can't. Thanks, though. Terrible cramps."

He makes a face and moves farther down the bar to ask someone else.

Do I know how to repulse a guy or what? I finish my wine and order another. Slow dance after slow dance. My friends keep right on dancing. Stupid sappy love songs. Don't people get that love hurts? You give your heart, and then he rips it right out of your chest. Without apology.

"Hello, Sydney," a crisp feminine voice says.

I immediately straighten my spine and pull my shoulders back. It's General Joan, Harper's grandmother. Her sharp brown eyes know all, see all. "Hello, Mrs. Ellis." Her short white hair is parted neatly to the side, and she's wearing a lacy lavender dress that ends below her knees. "You look lovely. It was a beautiful wedding."

"Yes, it was. What are you doing drinking at the bar instead of dancing?"

"Not in the mood. Can I get you a drink?"

"I had champagne earlier." She peers closely at me. "Your eyes are glassy. How many drinks have you had from this bar, young lady?"

"Only two." *Plus three more before the bar. Not sharing that.*

She grabs my glass. "And this is your third?"

"Uh, yeah. Hey!" She's walking away with my drink, limping a little from her bad hip. Do I chase her down? How bad would that look to chase down an elderly woman who stole my drink?

I watch as she takes it to a trash can behind the hot food bar and dumps it. Geez! Bit heavy-handed there. It's not like *I'm* her granddaughter. Though I have known her since I was five. She intimidated me from the start. Not anymore. I'm twenty-eight years old, and I'll order a drink if I feel like it.

I turn back to the bartender.

"Don't even think about it, young lady!" she barks, heading straight for me.

I cringe. The woman's voice carries, even above the music. People turn to stare at us. Harper sends me a beseeching look, begging me to take care of the situation. Garrett, her new husband, immediately strides toward General Joan, but she waves him off. He remains walking by her side until she reaches her destination—me.

"Mrs. Ellis would like you to stop at two drinks," Garrett dutifully reports.

"I got that," I say.

He checks in if she needs anything, and she sends him off to get her a "fancy shrimp puff."

"Drinking won't solve your problems," Mrs. Ellis informs me. "Harper told me you ended things with your fellow yesterday. You don't even have to tell me which young man he is. He's been staring at you since you walked down the aisle as bridesmaid at the church."

"He can stare all he wants," I say.

"He's in love with you, girl. Go talk to him. You think love comes along any day of the week?"

I give her a sideways look. "You don't understand. He wants to run my life."

She grips my arm. "I had a once-in-a-lifetime love to a wonderful man who left me too soon. Don't waste one precious moment."

I swallow hard. Her husband died when Harper was little. And my dad lost my mom too soon as well. He always said he was glad they married quickly because it meant he'd spent as much time as possible with her.

She sighs. "You don't have to kiss his ass. Just say hello, and things will progress from there."

I laugh a little. She rarely curses, so I know she's serious. "He's pissed I turned down his proposal the morning after accepting it, and I'm pissed he keeps going behind my back to fix my life. Which is going just fine, by the way, and would've been without his help."

She nods once. "So everybody's pissed and nobody's happy."

"Exactly," I say softly. She has a point. I'm miserable. I turn to look at Wyatt. He's standing next to a beautiful brunette actress. Her hand's on his arm, and he's not pushing it away. I recognize her from Harper's last TV show. He smiles down at her, saying something. I face front, a stab of jealousy making my chest ache.

"He seems just fine to me," I tell Mrs. Ellis. "I'm going to get a breath of fresh air."

I rush from the room, but not before I hear her say, "Foolish kids."

The icy wind whipping between buildings instantly sobers me up. Okay, he was just talking with that actress. Never mind that she's beautiful. What am I doing running away like this? I'm bold. I face life head-on. Mrs. Ellis is right. I should talk to him. I'll say hello. Maybe he'll apologize, and we can work it out.

Only when I return, he's slow dancing with the actress

from earlier. Pride and not a small amount of jealousy and indignation stop me in my tracks. We just broke up! You don't see me dancing with another guy. Mostly because I don't want another guy touching me right now. For Wyatt, it's no problem.

Screw it. I'm getting another glass of wine. I don't care what the General says. She never had to deal with the likes of Wyatt Winters.

It's now been three excruciating days since our breakup and not one word from him. Okay, he said hi as we passed each other on the way out of Harper's wedding reception, but that's it. No texts, no phone calls, nothing. Missing him is too much to bear alone. Thank God for my friends. I'm heading over to Jenna's apartment over Summerdale Sweets. She's most known for her cookies, brownies, and cupcakes. This past summer when she first opened the shop, her ice-cream sandwiches made with cake layers were wildly popular.

I ate a light dinner, knowing Jenna would provide decadent desserts. The moment I step inside her apartment, my mouth waters. It smells like chocolate heaven. My gaze darts to two bakery boxes sitting on the round glass table in the dining corner of the open living room. "Did you bring double fudge brownies?"

"Oh, hi, Jenna, so good to see you again," she says mockingly.

I laugh and give her a hug. "Sorry. I could really use the chocolate."

"Duh, of course I have the double fudge. What am I, new at ex recovery therapy?" She gestures to the boxes. "Help yourself. Audrey will be here any moment." She settles on her gray sectional sofa with throw pillows in red and black. Jenna's tall, so she picked a sofa you can stretch out on in one direction with a long chaise lounge on the side for another place to stretch out. The three of us have sprawled over that sofa many a night, sharing a bottle of wine and waxing philo-sophical about life, mostly men.

She's already set out small china plates for dessert. I peek in the box, torn between a salted caramel brownie and the double fudge. I glance over at her looking cozy in her light gray knit cap, gray cardigan over a cotton T-shirt, and jeans, her long legs tucked under her. "I can't decide."

She gestures toward the kitchen. "Get a knife and take a piece of as many goodies as you want. You don't want to eat multiple brownies, too rich even for you. You'll leave here with a stomachache."

I go to her small kitchen through an archway, grab a knife from the knife block, and go back for my brownies. I slice the salted caramel and double fudge in half and set them on a plate. I peek into the second box. Big fat homemade cookies—chocolate chunk, double chocolate chunk, butterscotch oatmeal, snickerdoodle, and peanut butter crunch. *Decisions, decisions.*

The doorbell rings, and Jenna pops off the sofa. "Audrey's here." She leaves to let Audrey in.

I grab a double chocolate chunk cookie, figuring the more chocolate, the better. I have so much food I just pull out one of the cushioned black leather chairs at the table and sit down. I don't want to get chocolate on her sofa.

"I brought the wine," Audrey says, appearing in the living room. Her long black hair stands out against her cream sweater that ends mid-thigh. She's in black yoga pants with sneakers. A more casual outfit for her. She often wears blouses with neat Peter Pan collars and trousers or a skirt to work.

"Hey," I say, giving her a small wave.

"How are you, Syd?" Her voice is full of sympathy, and my own throat closes with emotion. Chocolate is a temporary distraction. This breakup has been hard. I fell fast and broke up fast. It was a whirlwind that I'm still reeling from.

"Not great," I admit.

She sets two bottles of pinot grigio on the table, which is her favorite. I bet she brought them from home. She wraps an arm around me in a side hug, pressing her cheek against mine. "I see you've armed yourself well with chocolate."

"Yeah."

Jenna appears with a corkscrew and three wineglasses. "So how much do we hate Wyatt?" She uncorks the wine.

"I don't hate him," I say. "Gimme some wine, and I'll tell all." I only told them the basics before Harper's wedding on Saturday. The next day I was working.

Jenna pours a generous glass for me and then a normal portion for her and Audrey. She takes a seat on one side of me. Audrey is sitting on my other side, even closer. She pulled her chair over, probably so she could hug me as needed. We clink glasses in a silent *cheers* like we always do.

"What happened?" Audrey asks gently.

"Yeah, you seemed so happy with him," Jenna says. "We never saw you."

"You guys saw me almost every Thursday Night Wine Club," I say before shoving double fudge brownie in my mouth. I missed one Thursday night meeting when Wyatt and I went out for dinner in the city. I'm momentarily distracted by the explosion of rich chocolate flavor in my mouth. I could eat these all day.

"That was at The Horseman," Jenna says. "Not the three of us hanging out, or going out even. When's the last time we all went out?"

I swallow down brownie. "I'm too broke to go out, remember?" And now I'm in the clear thanks to Wyatt. No debt whatsoever. I wish I could appreciate that more. If only it wasn't wrapped up with so many strings. That's exactly why I did my own thing through Harper. And then he went behind my back *again*. He doesn't think I can handle being the boss of my own life. I've always been the boss.

"Oh, yeah," Audrey says. "We should plan something that's fun but free." She turns, giving me a meaningful look. "Do you need more wine and/or chocolate before sharing the details?"

I try to smile but can't quite pull it off. Then I spill my guts from the exhilarating high of love to the devastating low of a proposal made for all the wrong reasons.

They stare at me, open-mouthed in astonishment.

"I know!" I take a big bite of salted caramel brownie, the delicious sweetness temporarily soothing me.

Jenna and Audrey exchange a look.

"Did you know he proposed?" Jenna asks Audrey.

"No!" Audrey exclaims. "Syd! How could you not tell us this major news?"

I swallow the food in my mouth and chase it with a healthy portion of wine. "It just happened a few days ago, and we broke up right after, and then it was Harper's wedding, and yesterday I was working."

"Seriously?" Jenna says, narrowing her eyes at me. "We have known you forever and you keep this from us?"

My lower lip wobbles. "I was too devastated to say it out loud."

Audrey instantly wraps an arm around me, hugging me. "Okay, no problem. Sometimes it's hard to talk when you're upset, but in the future please know we don't care if you're blubbering your eyes out while choking out the words. We're here for you."

I do cry then, covering my face with my hands. Jenna rubs my back, murmuring sympathetically. Once the tears subside, I lift my head and sniffle. Jenna rushes off and returns with a tissue box.

"Thanks," I say, pulling a tissue out. I wipe my face dry and then blow my nose with another tissue.

Audrey holds her hand out for my used tissues. I laugh a little. "I'll do it." Audrey's such a nurturing person. She'll be a great mom one day.

I return from the kitchen to find my friends whispering to each other. "What?"

"Can we see the ring?" Jenna asks.

Audrey sips her wine, pretending she was never interested in the ring.

I flop down in my seat. "I left it there. He can propose to the next damsel in distress who needs rescuing. That's what he does, but that's not me. I rescue myself." I slash a hand in the air. "Already had. And then he blindsided me with his nefarious puppet-master plan."

Audrey nods sympathetically. "It was too soon for a proposal."

Jenna nods. "Only a couple of months ago you thought he was the most annoying—"

"Arrogant," Audrey corrects. "She thought he was arrogant. And evil."

"Satan," Jenna says.

His sister turned to him in despair, and he took care of her.

He brushes Snowball's teeth and grooms her daily after taking her in from an elderly neighbor.

He made me breakfast every morning.

My throat tightens, my eyes watering again. I take a swallow of wine.

"You can't propose just to sneak in gifts," Jenna declares.

Audrey sips her wine, not touching that one.

"It was a gift with strings," I tell Jenna.

"Did he ask to be part of your business?" Audrey asks.

I slap the table. "He said he automatically was since we'd be married."

Jenna cocks her head. "That's kinda true for most married couples, isn't it?"

My temper flares. "You're missing the point!"

Jenna's immediately contrite. "Sorry. He sucks."

"Totally," Audrey chimes in. "We hate him."

I sigh. "You don't have to hate him. He's not evil. He's just *wrong.*"

"So wrong," Audrey says soothingly.

I take a bite of double chocolate chunk cookie and chew, feeling marginally better. "So this is just how he is. I have to accept that. He fixes things. He's a fixer."

Audrey nods. "A man who fixes with misplaced intentions."

Jenna and Audrey exchange a look, which I pretend not to see. Something tells me they think I'm overreacting to Wyatt's big gesture. But it feels wrong to me. He wouldn't accept that

I can do stuff on my own, and I won't accept that he wants to be the big boss man who runs everyone's life. That's for his sisters and other failing businesses who ask for his help. I never asked. Well, I did ask for a loan before we were involved, but quickly nixed the idea when it was clear he wanted a piece of my restaurant.

I reach for more cookie, surprised I finished it. I was so lost in thought I didn't even notice I chowed down.

"Wyatt is like a repairman for your life," Audrey says thoughtfully. "But if you don't call the repairman to fix stuff, then it's an imposition." She lifts her palms. "Like, what are you doing in my house fixing stuff?"

"Exactly!" I exclaim. "That's exactly it. And he just wouldn't listen."

Jenna purses her lips. "Despicable."

"Not that bad." I feel obligated to scale back on how horrible he is. That's not the man I know, though I appreciate the support. "He had good intentions. It's just I didn't need or want a repairman, like Audrey said. He offered to help, and I turned him down. But then he went behind my back to Drew and then Harper."

"Let's get Harp in on this," Jenna says, pulling out her phone.

"No," I say. "Isn't she in Aruba on her honeymoon?"

Jenna taps her phone. "They leave tomorrow. She had an appointment today she didn't want to miss at the obstetrician. They're finding out the sex of the baby."

"Put her on speakerphone," Audrey says.

I finish my wine in one long swallow. I love Harp to death, but I don't expect her to understand. She thinks Wyatt's awesome. She's the one who accepted his offer to pay off my loan as an engagement present. She knew before I did that he was going to propose and exactly what he was up to. She should've told me. Knowing Harp, she probably thought it was romantic. She's so gaga for Garrett she wants everyone to be in love like they are. It's not that easy for some of us.

Harper's warm voice rings out. "Hi, ladies, drum roll, please."

I dutifully drum roll on the table.

"It's a girl!" she exclaims.

We all cheer and congratulate her.

"We're having wine and chocolate in your honor," Audrey says.

"Thanks," Harper says with a laugh. "We're both so happy. I'm going to shop for some cute girly outfits on our honeymoon."

"So sorry to bother you," I say. "You must be packing and getting ready."

"Nope. Just relaxing at home. It's not a bother. I thought you called to find out about the baby."

I wince. In my own misery, I forgot about her big news. "Yes, but also Jenna wanted to check in with you on my, uh, personal situation."

"Oh," she says. "Are you doing okay?"

"Awful," Jenna says. "Wyatt proposed just to fix Sydney's life, which did not need any help, thank you very much."

I shove her. "Don't make fun. I have a legit reason to be mad."

"What happened?" Harper asks.

Audrey fills her in on all the facts: He proposed. He paid off my loan. We fought and broke up over his heavy-handedness. He went behind my back twice.

We all stare at the phone on the table, waiting for Harper's opinion.

"Syd, he can come off the wrong way sometimes, not always choosing the best way to express himself, but I know deep down he's a good guy." Harper pauses. "I thought it was a romantic engagement gift. Didn't he tell you that's what it was?"

"Yes, but I didn't want him tangled up in my business. And he swore he wouldn't interfere if I didn't ask, which I didn't." A fresh wave of anger pours through me. I need my friends to understand why what he did was wrong. "He thinks he has to rescue me when I can damn well rescue myself!"

"And you broke up over it," Harper says. "It's a shame

you can't just be together without being engaged. Do you think you could maybe take a step back, regroup, and go back to the way it was before the, uh, unwanted proposal?"

"No," I say. "Because he doesn't see that what he did was wrong, so that means he'll keep doing it. Jumping in to fix my life without my asking for help." My voice cracks, and I take a sip of Audrey's wine since mine is gone. She rubs my back sympathetically.

"Oh, Syd," Harper says.

"I don't need a man to make my life work," I say. "I can do it on my own."

"She cried earlier," Jenna says.

My eyes get hot. I don't cry easily. My friends know it.

"I wish I could be there right now," Harper says. "I feel like you need a big group hug."

"I'm fine," I say. "I *will* be fine. You just enjoy your honeymoon. We'll get together when you get back."

Her life sounds charmed compared to mine. And I know she works hard, but I work hard too, and I feel like I'm nowhere near where I thought I'd be by my age. I was supposed to have a cool apartment, a serious boyfriend, and a savings account big enough to let me go out with my friends without worrying about paying for a night out.

I thank her, and we all say our goodbyes.

Audrey turns to me. "Would it help if he apologized?"

"He won't," I say. "He doesn't think he did anything wrong."

They're quiet for a moment.

I pour myself another glass of wine. "Enough about me. What's going on in your love lives?"

"I slept with the delivery guy this afternoon," Jenna says, her green eyes sparkling.

"Jenna!" Audrey and I exclaim in near unison.

"The delivery guy?" I ask, biting into a rich chocolate brownie.

Jenna wiggles her fingers in the air, smiling. "It's been building for a while now, flirting, long gazes, you know. His name is Trey, and that's all I know about him."

"Now what?" Audrey asks. "Are you going to keep seeing him?"

"Is this going to be a daily hookup?" I ask. "Deliver the flour, sugar, and eggs, and get in me, Trey!"

Jenna laughs. "No, I told him it was a onetime thing. We agreed up front. You know I don't want anything serious."

"Why not?" Audrey asks. "I just don't get it. Don't you ever think about the future, getting married, settling down?"

"After my parents' nasty divorce?" Jenna asks. "The last thing I want is to be married."

"Well, I want that," Audrey says, staring at the table. "Someday."

"You've been so cool toward Drew," I say. "Usually you always give him a warm hello at the bar. What's up with that?"

Audrey blushes. "I say hello."

I shake my head. "Not like you used to. Come on, it's us."

She smiles tightly. "Absolutely nothing happened." She sighs. "Jenna, you should try not to let your parents' divorce affect your choices. You deserve to be happy."

Jenna gives her a deadpan stare. "It was a nightmare. A drawn-out battle with my sister and me caught in the middle. Hard pass."

"I need to meet a man," Audrey says.

Jenna and I exchange a wide-eyed look of surprise. "Go, Audrey!" I say, socking her on the shoulder.

"Get it, girl," Jenna says. "But you're going to have to branch out beyond Summerdale. Slim pickings. Ooh, check out this new app." She taps and shows her the screen.

Audrey pushes it away. "I'm not looking for a hookup. I'd like someone looking for a serious relationship. A guy who reads preferably."

That's definitely not Drew. He never liked to read growing up.

"Ooh, there's Hot Guys Who Read," Jenna says, showing Audrey her phone screen again. "It's just a social media account, but I bet some of them are single. And these pictures are all from New York City."

Audrey looks to me. "Let me know if a guy comes into The Horseman Inn that looks like a literary type. Otherwise, I'm going to try eLoveMatch."

We both stare at her. For so long, she was opposed to online dating. That app is for people serious about a relationship. She's finally moving on from Drew, her lifelong crush. It was love at first sight for her when she was the tender age of six. He was eleven and obsessed with sports, barely noticing my friends. I thought she'd grow out of it, but she's always only had eyes for him. Once he signed up for the army, Audrey asked to write him when he was away. I think they became friends of a sort, email pen pals more like. In any case, when he came home, they were friends. Sure, she dated a bit in high school and college, but never for long. No one could ever live up to Drew.

"I'll do it with you," I tell her.

Audrey's brows knit over concerned eyes. "It's too soon for you."

"That's okay," I say, nudging her shoulder. "I figure it'll take you a while to actually follow through."

"Busted!" Jenna says.

We laugh, even Audrey. "I'm serious this time," she says. "I'm going for it. It's time."

For some reason that makes us laugh even harder. Audrey huffs and tosses cookie pieces at us.

I grab the cookie from where it landed on my shirt and pop it in my mouth. "No wasting cookie."

Audrey gets serious. "I'm still hopeful for you, Syd. If he apolog—"

"Nope," I say.

"Grovel," Jenna says. "If he grovels at your feet."

I point at Jenna. "Except he never will. Wyatt Winters is all knowing, all powerful, always one hundred percent right."

Except this time I'm one hundred percent right.

20

Sydney

Welp, it's been two weeks, and I calmed down enough to spend some time thinking about the future of The Horseman Inn, and Wyatt's idea of a farm-to-table angle is something I'd like to do. What could be better than having farm-fresh produce and meat, along with freshly caught fish? This area is plentiful with the ocean only an hour drive away and many local farms. I called around, looking for some suppliers, and got a lot of good leads. Only problem is when I mentioned the idea to our longtime chef, George, he took offense. He's not a "frou-frou fancy chef" he declared. He's a comfort chef. And then he informed me if I went through with it, he'd quit.

Now George is a family friend, in his sixties, and has been with The Horseman Inn since my dad took it over from my grandfather. Obviously I don't want to lose him, but this is a business, and sometimes you have to make hard business decisions. I didn't fire him, but I'm meeting a potential chef at a coffee shop near the Culinary Institute of America, an hour's drive away in Hyde Park, New York. Darren's graduating this spring, which means he's eager for work and full of new ideas. We already spoke over the phone, and he sounds like a great fit. He even grew up not far from here, so it would be like coming home. I've kept it under wraps, but if it works out, it'll give George plenty of time to find a new job. It's the end of February now, and Darren wouldn't start until May.

I get everything ready for Friday trivia night, planning to leave it in the hands of our bartender Betsy before I leave for my chef interview. I'm excited about taking this step for The Horseman Inn. It's the first thing I've done that wasn't just treading water, desperately trying to keep the place afloat.

"Sydney," a deep baritone voice says urgently.

My head whips toward Wyatt, and I step out from behind the bar. "What's wrong?" His dark hair is disheveled, his eyes wild.

"She ran away. I can't find her anywhere."

I rush over to him. "Who? Kayla?"

"No, not Kayla! Snowball!" He shoves a hand in his hair. "With the construction, there's an open wall. The crew stapled plastic sheets over it, but there must've been a gap. She got out, and I've searched the whole property. It'll be dark soon, and she's so little she just blends in with the hills and trees. Can you help me look for her?"

He came to me for help. The man who fixes everyone else's problems needs *me*. Oh shit. I'm supposed to leave in a few minutes to interview Darren. He told me he has several interviews lined up. If I miss it, someone else might snatch him up. Darren worked for a big-name chef before deciding to take the plunge and go for formal training at the Culinary Institute. In other words, he's a catch. On the other hand, Wyatt needs me. Snowball needs me. The poor thing is stuck somewhere in the cold of winter in unfamiliar terrain. She might not survive the night.

"Just give me a minute."

He surprises me, grabbing me in a quick hug. "Thank you."

"Of course." I quickly let Betsy know what's going on and give her instructions for trivia night.

I meet up with him. "Let's go."

He heads for the door, his long legs eating up the space. I have to hurry to keep up with him.

Once we're in his car, I ask, "Is Kayla looking for her too?"

"No, she's in the city, visiting our sister. I didn't even notice Snowball was gone for more than an hour. She could be anywhere. She could be eaten by one of those coyotes howling away in the woods!"

If his little dog is in the woods, it's a very real possibility she could've been taken by a coyote. They hunt in packs and have gotten more comfortable with suburbia, hunting in the daytime as well as night.

"We'll find her," I say.

His jaw is tight, his eyes focused on the road as he speeds back to his house.

"Take it slow when we get close to the house in case she's out there and you don't see her at first."

He slows down. "Right. You're right. Can you imagine if I ran her over after trying to rescue her?" His voice is shaky. "She's just so little and helpless. She doesn't know anything about the country. She's used to one city block."

The sun's starting to set, and I estimate we've got a half hour to find her before it's dark. "Will she come if you call her?"

"She does. She always does. She must be far away or stuck somewhere. For all I know, she fell down a well. Anything could've happened."

"It's okay. We'll find her."

He drives the rest of the way in grim silence. I text a message to Darren, cancelling on him and apologizing for the last minute. He texts back: *ok*. That's it. Just ok.

Me: *I'll be in touch.*

Darren: *ok.*

Not much of a communicator by text, but I didn't want to call when Wyatt's so upset and driving way too fast.

He abruptly hits the brakes as he turns into his driveway, the car fishtailing for a moment on the freshly falling snow, and slowly drives up the rest of the way. We had a warm spell this past week, and the snow had mostly melted, but it's snowing again, the wind whipping it around.

"Do you have any meat?" I ask. "That might draw her out."

"I was using her biscuits, but that's a good idea. I have some deli meat. Roast beef. She's always sniffing around for scraps of that." His eyes water for a moment, and then he parks and darts out of the car.

I follow him into the house. It's weird being here now two weeks after our breakup. The living room floor is finished now. I get a flashback to last time—the bouquet of roses, his smile as he greeted me at the door. *No, don't go there.*

I join him in the kitchen. "Microwave the meat for a bit so the scent carries more."

"Good idea." He throws a pile of roast beef into the microwave and stands, hands on hips, waiting for it to finish. The microwave dings, and he grabs the meat, giving me half before leading the way toward the back of the house. "This is where they're building the room out to include a powder room. I thought she wandered out to the backyard. Look how much space she could've gotten lost in."

There's tons of land, rolling hills edged by thick forest.

"Did you see any paw prints?" I ask.

"No. The falling snow must've covered them." He leads the way out the front door. "We'll use the flashlights on our phones if it gets dark. Just keep calling her name." He looks around as soon as he gets outside. "Snowball, come!"

Silence.

"Does she have a name tag on her collar?" I'm hoping if someone finds her, they can get her back to Wyatt.

"Yes, but it has my old number in the city on it. Shit." He heads around toward the back of the house, waving the roast beef in the air and calling her name.

If I were a short city dog facing cold and unfamiliar terrain, where would I go? She's used to short walks through the woods with Kayla. But alone? I think she'd seek shelter close by. I walk the perimeter around the house, calling her name, and then go to the lighthouse structure. There's a door, but it's locked. I don't think she could've squeezed under it.

I crouch on the ground, looking at the world from her size. Maybe under a bush. I look all around his yard while Wyatt tromps through the woods, yelling her name. I start calling her too, adding a whistle in case that carries better. I glance toward the busy road at the end of his long driveway and pray she didn't go in that direction. I'm sure she'd be run over by a car. It would be easy for a driver not to see her. That's a last resort place to look. Because if she's run over, there's nothing we can do for her anyway. I don't think a dog that small would survive it.

"Snowball!" I call. "Snowball, come!" I slap my knee and then add a whistle.

I search until it's dark, and then stop and sit on Wyatt's front porch, turning on the flashlight on my phone. It's below freezing, and I'm getting really cold. I don't think she'll survive the night. I can hear Wyatt's increasingly desperate calls from the back of the house. And then I hear something else, a snuffling sound. An animal is nearby, probably interested in the hunk of roast beef I'm holding. It could be any number of creatures—raccoon, mole, even a coyote.

I get off the porch and aim my light under the porch. There's a lattice wood barrier, making it hard to see. "Snowball, is that you?" I can't see much but dirt. I walk around, looking for any gaps where a dog might've gotten through. And then I find it, behind a hedge on the side of the porch, there's a small gap in the lattice wood. I get down on my stomach and aim my flashlight. Two sets of eyes shine back at me. "Snowball! What are you doing under there? Who's your friend?" Snowball is curled up with a skinny pit bull. "Who wants meat?"

I text Wyatt that I found her. I can't fit in the small space, but I'm hoping to coax them out. I roll up a piece of roast beef and stick it through the gap as far as my arm will go. I tense in case the pit bull is a biter, ready to yank my arm back, but it's Snowball who trots over. I pull back, coaxing her closer. "That's right, come get the yummy roast beef."

As soon as she's in reach, I grab her, pulling her out and letting her bite a piece of roast beef off. I toss the rest in for her friend.

"Oh my God, you found her." Wyatt crouches down next

to us and takes Snowball. "You scared the crap out of me," he scolds her. "Stupid move. Don't ever do that again."

"There's another dog under your porch. I think it's a stray."

He looks. "No collar. He's seen better days. You think he's dangerous?"

"Snowball didn't think so. She was curled up against him."

"How long do you think he was under there?"

"No idea."

He breaks off roast beef and tosses a trail of meat towards the opening. "Come on, guy. Follow the trail."

"How're you going to get him inside without a collar?"

"He'll either follow me or go back where he came from."

The dog shuffles forward on his belly and gingerly takes a piece of meat.

"Look how slow he eats," I whisper.

"He's cautious. Probably came from a rough situation." He waits patiently, Snowball tucked into his jacket, coaxing the stray dog to take more meat. As soon as he does, Wyatt tosses a piece just outside the opening.

"Come on, Rex, little further," he coaxes.

"Rex?"

"He looks like a Rex, doesn't he?"

He's already named him. That's Wyatt. Taking care of everyone.

Rex finally ventures out and takes the meat.

I stifle a cheer in case it scares him away.

"Rex, come," Wyatt orders and heads for the front door. I follow him, but Rex doesn't.

We get inside, and Wyatt keeps the door open, waving the meat at Rex. "Meat for you. Come."

Rex looks undecided, and then Snowball barks, and it's decided. Rex trots inside and gobbles up another slice of roast beef. I quickly shut the door behind him.

Wyatt turns to me. "Syd, thank you."

"I take care of those I love," I say, using his words to me from before.

He sets Snowball down, tosses the rest of the meat to the dogs, and kisses me.

It's like coming home again.

21

───────

Wyatt

That night, Sydney and I have a "heart-to-heart" talk. Her words. I solemnly vow not to take over and solve her problems for her. And she solemnly vows to ask for help when she needs it. This is a serious conversation we have behind closed doors in my room, which I like because I know what comes next—makeup sex.

We're sitting side by side on the mattress, pressed up close together, shoulder to shoulder, thigh to thigh, holding hands. I squeeze her hand. "We good now?"

She gives me a long hard look. "As long as you understand what you did wrong going behind my back and fixing stuff."

That's the second time she said that, and I realize she wants an apology before moving on. I'm just happy she's here with me, pressed up against my side. It's a good sign when your serious talk happens with all this touching.

I lift our joined hands and brush a kiss over her knuckles. "I went about it wrong. I'm sorry. I love you, Syd, you must know I did it out of love. I don't want you to suffer when you don't have to. I want you to be happy."

"I was happy before, so happy with you, and with the

way things were starting to turn around at work." She sighs. "Please just always be up front with me, okay? That's a deal breaker. No going behind my back to fix things. We can fix stuff together from here on out. I can help you with stuff too. We'll help each other out."

A rush of affection has me hugging her and kissing her cheek. I've been taking care of everyone else for so long it never occurred to me someone would take care of me. Wouldn't that be a relief to get a break for once?

"Deal," I say. "Now let's get naked." I tackle her to the mattress and she laughs, her arms going around my neck.

I nuzzle into her neck, breathing her in. I lift my head, gazing at her beautiful face. "I missed you so much."

She blinks back tears, running her fingers through my hair. "I missed you too. It was awful. Let's never be apart again."

"Never."

She hugs me tight for a long moment and then shoves me off her, getting off the bed completely. She strips out of her work T-shirt, jeans, and sneakers. She gestures toward me. "What are you waiting for?"

"You're so beautiful," I say reverently.

She tugs my shirt off. "I was promised wild monkey sex if we partnered up."

"You want me in your business?"

She gives me a sexy smile. "Among other places." She gets into bed and crooks her finger at me.

My chest puffs with pride. She trusts me in all things. She loves me. I'm so damn lucky.

I strip in no time, roll a condom on, and join her. I cover her, kissing her tenderly. Within moments, the kiss turns urgent, our bodies eager to join after too long apart.

My mind clouds, nothing but intense need. Hands stroking, mouths hungry, her nails scraping down my back.

My name from her lips over and over.

Pumping harder, faster, impossible to stop.

I gaze into her eyes, that deep connection electrifying me for a timeless moment.

"Marry me," she whispers.

She arches her hips up, tightening around me, and I'm gone, my release rushing through me, only dimly aware of her soft moans.

I collapse on top of her, breathing hard as the world slowly comes into focus. *She proposed to me.*

I lift my head and kiss her. "Be right back."

She smiles and hums her reply.

I'm not wasting any time. I retrieve what I need from my duffel bag, join her in the bed, and slide it on her finger.

She lifts her hand with the diamond engagement ring I saved in the hope that one day we'd be together. She beams. "I didn't think you heard me."

"I couldn't speak at the time. I think that might be a first—sexual climax proposal."

"Is that a yes?" she asks, her eyes sparkling.

I slide under the covers with her and wrap an arm around her. She curls into my side. "Yes, my she-devil, I will marry you."

"And?"

"And be your partner in all things with everything up front as we help each other."

"Good."

"And?" I prompt. "What will you be? Hint. It involves being naked." I'm talking about getting her pregnant. A gift we give each other. I'm such a romantic.

"And I will be your sex slave?"

I chuckle and kiss her. "Don't think I won't hold you to that. It's going right into the wedding vows. Sydney Robinson promises to be my loving wife, partner, and sex slave."

She strokes my beard and kisses me. "I love you."

My throat clogs with emotion. "I love you too."

She props up on an elbow. "Are you crying?"

"No."

"Your eyes are watering."

I rub my watery eyes. "I was just thinking how I wanted

you to be the mother of my children, and you said sex slave, and they're both perfect."

Her eyes well. "Oh, Wyatt." She squeezes me around the middle and then shifts back to look at me, love shining in her eyes. "I'll never let you go. You'll always be in my heart."

"Syd." I kiss her gently. "You are my heart."

EPILOGUE

A sunny day in May...

Sydney

I'm about to marry my best friend. I always dreamed of meeting a man who would be a true partner in my life, with the added bonus of an awesome sex life. I just never thought it would be to the man who challenged me at every turn. But I'm better for it, and I think he's better off because of me too. It's a relief for him to know I can take the reins on a project instead of him having to take care of everything. For example, our wedding—all me. The honeymoon—all him. And together we've brought The Horseman Inn back from the dead.

I own the place, and it's mine to pass down to our children. I manage it and handle the marketing and the books. Wyatt consults with his ideas and has taken a special interest in the bar. He's spent a lot of time finding local breweries to expand our beer list, which is attracting beer connoisseurs. We've also toured local vineyards in the Finger Lakes of New York to add more selections to our wine list, which has created a lot of buzz through my Thursday Night Wine Club. And gotten a lot of people buzzed. Ha-ha. I add fun cocktails seasonally to the bar menu and make sure to stock a selection of quality whiskies—his favorite. He's so jazzed about all the fine drink selections that he'll sometimes work behind the bar, alongside Betsy, and recommend things to customers, singing the praises of every personally chosen beer, wine, or whiskey.

My man.

That chef I was hoping to bring on board slipped through my fingers, lured away by a fancy Manhattan restaurant. Wyatt wanted to lure him back with a higher salary—he felt responsible since I missed the interview to help him—but I said no. He probably wouldn't have been happy at The Horseman Inn for long. It all worked out. Now we have Spencer, who apprenticed under a chef at a farm-to-table restaurant. No fancy culinary school degree, but the customers enjoy his food, which is all that matters. Our old chef, George, went to the diner in town, a small place next to the gas station dating from the 1950s. His style of comfort food is appreciated there.

"It's time," Jenna says.

I sniffle and wipe under my eyes, careful not to smudge my makeup. I'm getting ready in the master bathroom of Wyatt's home, which is now mine too. He told me to choose whatever I wanted for the master bath because he wanted me to feel comfortable. I chose a double sink with a vanity between where I could sit and get ready. There's also a whirlpool soaking tub and a separate shower. It's luxurious, and I thought at first it would feel weird. It's strange how quickly you can get used to luxury. I never take it for granted though.

"Don't start crying," Jenna says, peering over my shoulder in the vanity mirror. "You have to look put together at least until you make it down the aisle."

"Oh, I can't look," Audrey says, waving a hand in front of her face. "It'll get me all teary too."

"I'm ready," I say, standing in my gown. I'm not a pretty princess type of bride—no veil or huge train or poufy layers. Despite choosing a silk strapless sheath gown that drapes to my ankles, I feel sort of magical wearing it. Not exactly a princess. More like…a goddess.

"So pretty!" Audrey exclaims. "This is the perfect gown for you."

"Thank you."

I step into the master bedroom, where Harper is relaxing on a chaise lounge with her feet up. She's only a few weeks from her due date, and her ankles are swollen. She opted out of the bridal party because she didn't want to be on her feet more than she had to. "Syd! You're stunning! Wyatt's eyes will pop out of his head."

"I hope not," I say with a smile.

She works her way to sitting upright and prepares to stand. Jenna rushes over to help. "I'm sorry I couldn't do more," Harper says as she stands with some assistance. "You know I'm here for you." She walks over and hugs me, her huge belly pressing between us.

I pull back, holding her by the arms, and stare at her belly under a peach maternity dress. "How's Joan Junior doing in there?" That's her grandmother's name. I'm teasing, picking up on what her husband, Garrett, always says.

She rubs her belly with a content smile. "This one is going to have a name all her own. We're going to wait until she's born to see what name fits. She was just kicking up a storm, but now that I'm on the move, I think she'll settle."

I look at my three best friends, whom I've known since we were girls huddled together on the playground. "You guys! I'm so glad you're with me on this special day. First Harper ties the knot, now me." I give Jenna and Audrey a watery smile. "I can't wait to be at your weddings too!"

"Okay, hug and let's go," Jenna says dryly. She's not one for big emotional displays. I don't usually have emotional displays either. It's just that I love them so much and I love Wyatt so much and this is just a momentous day.

I give her a quick hug, and then Audrey, and one more for Harper before I walk ahead, leading the way to the family room at the back of the house. It was an addition beyond the library, a casual space for our future family. The back of the room is a wall of floor-to-ceiling windows with double patio doors leading to the outside.

There's a small white canopy for our ceremony in the backyard, with rows of chairs draped in white. Another large tent farther back is ready for the reception, with tables and chairs surrounding a dance floor and a head table for the bridal party. It's all very elegant. Full confession: I leaned on Kayla to help with the details. She was way into the wedding planning, and it took some of the pressure off me when I got caught up in work. We're close, and she loves Summerdale so much, she wanted to stay. Wyatt says it's the tamales that sold her, but I suspect it was my brother Adam. They got to talking while he was working on the custom carpentry work in Wyatt's library, as well as in the living room. She insists they're just friends, and she's not looking for a relationship. She's healing right now. (Though it's been four months since she was dumped at the altar.)

She finished her thesis a couple of weeks ago, and while she's looking for a job, I hired her as a waitress at The Horseman Inn. She's great with memorizing orders, even when they get complicated, and she's *really* trying not to drop dishes. I told her she could continue living with me and Wyatt, but she insisted newly married couples need their space. Now she lives in my old apartment above the restaurant.

Everyone's in place. Wyatt's talking to his groomsmen, laughing. His best man is a former business partner I recently met, along with Garrett, Harper's husband, as groomsman.

The moment my friends and I appear at the end of the red runner aisle, Garrett springs into action, striding down the aisle to Harper. He guides her to a front-row seat next to her grandmother, the wise General Joan. She told me not to waste time being miserable apart from Wyatt, and she was right.

Wyatt's eyes meet mine, and my heart thumps hard. Even from this distance I can see the emotion take over his face, his eyes watery. My eyes well too. *My gorgeous groom.*

～

Wyatt

My beautiful bride. I'm about to marry my true love, the woman I can't wait to spend the rest of my life with. I love everything about her. She's smart, funny, and just fiery enough to banter with me instead of taking offense. And I'm a better man because of her. I'm learning to let go of taking over and solving problems for everyone. I mean, I'm good at it, but now I only step in when asked. And Sydney only asks when she's exhausted every option and is at a standstill. We help each other out.

Audrey and then Jenna walk down the aisle. Sydney waits her turn, her arm linked in her older brother Drew's, who's standing in for her dad. I'll do the same for my sisters. Drew looks serious in his navy suit, his back ramrod straight, shoulders back, looking like the soldier he used to be. I like him. He's grumpy, but I can get him to crack a smile now and then.

I glance over at Snowball and Rexie (formerly known as Rex, turns out she's a girl dog) in matching pink collars. We put up signs around town for Rexie and had her checked for a microchip, but no one claimed her, so I did. Snowball has a small white lacy bow on top of her head. *Not* my idea. Kayla dressed them for the occasion. They're lying at her feet in the front row.

My gaze returns to Sydney. It's such a relief to have someone you know can get stuff done by your side so it's not all on you. Like when I was at my wit's end, trying to take care of Rexie. She just would *not* get comfortable with me. We think she had a bad experience with a man. So Sydney took over, taking care of Rexie and training her with a few simple commands. Rexie tolerates me now. She worships Sydney.

The wedding march begins, and I stand straighter, a lump in my throat. I watch my future wife approach, my gaze riveted on her smiling face. She's looking at our friends and family as she goes down the aisle, until finally she locks those beautiful honey brown eyes on me. My heart thumps harder, my throat tightening. *My bride.*

A few moments later, her brother releases her to me. I take her hand in mine and dip my head to her ear. "Beautiful."

She squeezes my hand, and we turn to the minister. I barely hear what the guy's saying, I'm so enthralled with Sydney. Her auburn hair falls in waves over her strapless gown. Her face looks nearly angelic as she listens, though I know better. She can be quite wicked in every way that I love. She looks as content and happy as I feel.

Finally, it's time for the vows, and I speak up loud and clear, holding both of her hands in mine. "I promise to love, honor, and cherish you for the rest of my days." She smiles, her eyes dancing, and I know she's thinking of our joking sex-slave vows. I smile back and squeeze her hands. "And I promise to ask for help when I need it."

Everyone laughs.

I turn to our family and friends. "It's important." We broke up over it, so I had to get it into the vows. This is a forever deal.

More titters from the crowd.

Sydney beams at me. And then she promises the same.

Next thing, I know it's official. I frame her face in my hands and kiss her tenderly before wrapping my arms around her in a hug.

"We did it," she whispers.

I pull back to look at her. "And it wasn't that hard either."

We grin at each other and then head down the aisle, the sounds of applause and whistles ringing out.

After a brief break for pictures, including Snowball and Rexie, of course, we join everyone for the reception. Tuxedoed waiters are circulating with champagne and appetizers.

The band is playing cheerful swing music in the background. Sydney looks up at me. "We should've taken dance lessons for our first dance. I knew I forgot something."

"It's easy. Just sway back and forth."

"I think we're supposed to do something more than that. Everyone will be watching."

I tip her chin up and kiss her. "I'll just make out with you as a distraction technique."

She narrows her eyes.

"No?" I wrap my arms around her waist. "Allow me to

demonstrate." I sway a bit and feign going in for a sloppy kiss.

She pushes me away, laughing. "Okay, we'll do the slow sway and that's it. No sexy stuff on the dance floor."

"It's not like they don't know we're about to get it on tonight."

She pulls me close. "Shh."

"In a honeymoon suite in the city with a vibrating bed."

Her eyes widen. "You did *not* book us a hotel with a vibrating bed."

I smirk. "The person in charge of the honeymoon gets to pick the details."

She relaxes. "Very funny. Where are we going for our honeymoon?"

"Did you pack your bikinis?"

She looks to the sky before looking back at me. "Yes, I packed the six ridiculous string bikinis you bought me, along with the comfortable tankini I bought myself."

"Hmm," I say, briefly considering saying I threw out her tankini. The potential shout of outrage might not be appropriate on this happy occasion. Not that I did. But wouldn't it be funny to say so?

"Hmm, what?"

"You have all you need for our honeymoon—your groom and your six stunning bikinis." I kiss her cheek. "You make them stunning, my beautiful bride."

She blushes. "Thank you."

"Though I'm not sure you need them. There are nude beaches."

"Is it in Europe?"

"At the water park," I finish.

She laughs and then stops abruptly. "Beelzebub?"

"Yes, she-devil?"

"If we're going to a water park full of screaming kids, you're going to need to plan a second honeymoon."

I smile mysteriously. We're actually going to Bora Bora in French Polynesia and staying at an amazing five-star resort. I can't help but play with her.

She wags her finger at me. "I'll get it out of you soon."

"You might need to use some of your sexy charm on me. Naked."

"I won't need to be naked. I will figure it out based on every hint you drop."

She thinks she can outsmart me. *Game on.* I barely resist rubbing my hands together. She's just so fun.

I hold up admirably, if I do say so myself. Sydney keeps working on me when I least expect it. During our first dance, she says, "I want to dance on our honeymoon with mariachi players in the background."

She thinks it's Mexico because of my love of Mexican food.

"Anything you want," I answer mysteriously.

While we slice the cake together, she says, "I'll come back with no tan lines from our tropical honeymoon in the Caribbean."

"That's because you don't tan," I reply. "You'll look cute in a Goofy hat."

That throws her off the Caribbean line of thinking.

Now we're slow dancing along with a lot of other couples. I'm holding her close, pressed right up against me, half hugging, half lusting for my bride. Her arms are around my neck as we move in a slow sway.

"Are there spinning teacups there?" she asks.

Ha! Now she's thinking we're going to Happy Mouse Land full of rides and water park attractions.

"I probably should've asked about that," I say. "That would be cool to see spinning teacups."

She grumbles something I don't catch. I chuckle to myself.

Harper and Garrett are dancing nearby. He's leading in a waltz, guiding her from a distance, her belly between them. It's the first time they've been out on the dance floor. She whispers something to him, and they leave. She needs frequent bathroom breaks. With them out of the way, I see something odd.

Kayla is dancing with Sydney's older brother Adam. Too close. I thought they were just friends. Kayla prefers nerdy academic types. He's tall and lean with muscle and looks different now in a suit than in his usual T-shirt and jeans with a toolbelt. Handsome in the way Kayla likes, more clean-cut, though he still has the usual dark brown scruff on his jaw. Kayla was constantly pestering him while he was trying to work at my place. I told her to let the poor man do his job.

"Are there nude beaches on the Amalfi coast?" Sydney asks.

Kayla runs her fingers through Adam's dark brown hair. His eyes lock on hers. What the—

Sydney pokes me in the ribs.

"Yeah," I answer distractedly. "I made sure of that."

Kayla goes up on tiptoe to whisper something in Adam's ear. *What is she saying?*

"So we're going to Italy?" Sydney asks.

Adam looks alarmed. I'm alarmed. *What is my baby sister doing? Propositioning him?*

"Wyatt," Sydney prompts, "could you possibly pay attention to your bride on our wedding day?"

I tear my gaze away and focus on her. "It's not Italy." I glance back at Kayla and Adam, but they're gone.

"I could use your help," Sydney purrs in my ear.

I hear the hint of seduction in her voice, and lust rushes through my body, robbing my mind of coherent thought. I grab her hand. "I know just the place."

She laughs as I take her back to the house for a little private time. We lock ourselves in the library.

And then we help each other out. Exactly as promised.

Would you like to read about Wyatt and Sydney's honeymoon? Sign up for my newsletter for a special Bonus Epilogue! https://www.kyliegilmore.com/FGnewsletter

Don't miss the next book in the series, *Dashing*, where Adam gets an unusual request from Kayla.

Dashing

Adam

True or false? Men and women can't be friends. I used to say true, until I met Kayla.

Yes, she's a goddess, but it's completely platonic. So when she asks me to pose as her fiancé at a party, I'm all in. Especially since her sleazeball ex will be there. Can you believe this weasel dumped her at the altar? I've got your back, Kayla. What are friends for?

But now I'm worried I played the part too well because we're heading home, and she makes a confession: she's tired of saving herself for marriage and wants me to be her first. *Her first!*

I can't go there. The woman has committed relationship written all over her, something I'm never doing again for good reason.

Except when I tell her no, she starts considering other candidates. I can't let her be with some random guy! I can't cross the line either. She doesn't know what she's asking! She doesn't know what she's doing! Someone has to stop her.

Kayla

Only Adam will do.

ALSO BY KYLIE GILMORE

Unleashed Romance <<steamy romcoms with dogs!

Fetching (Book 1)

Dashing (Book 2)

Sporting (Book 3)

**Happy Endings Book Club Series <<the Campbell family and a
romance book club collide!**

Hidden Hollywood (Book 1)

Inviting Trouble (Book 2)

So Revealing (Book 3)

Formal Arrangement (Book 4)

Bad Boy Done Wrong (Book 5)

Mess With Me (Book 6)

Resisting Fate (Book 7)

Chance of Romance (Book 8)

Wicked Flirt (Book 9)

An Inconvenient Plan (Book 10)

A Happy Endings Wedding (Book 11)

The Clover Park Series <<brothers who put family first!

The Opposite of Wild (Book 1)

Daisy Does It All (Book 2)

Bad Taste in Men (Book 3)

Kissing Santa (Book 4)

Restless Harmony (Book 5)

Not My Romeo (Book 6)

Rev Me Up (Book 7)

An Ambitious Engagement (Book 8)

Clutch Player (Book 9)

A Tempting Friendship (Book 10)

Clover Park Bride: Nico and Lily's Wedding

A Valentine's Day Gift (Book 11)

Maggie Meets Her Match (Book 12)

The Clover Park STUDS series <<hawt geeks who unleash into studs!

Almost Over It (Book 1)

Almost Married (Book 2)

Almost Fate (Book 3)

Almost in Love (Book 4)

Almost Romance (Book 5)

Almost Hitched (Book 6)

The Rourkes Series <<swoonworthy princes and kickass princesses!

Royal Catch (Book 1)

Royal Hottie (Book 2)

Royal Darling (Book 3)

Royal Charmer (Book 4)

Royal Player (Book 5)

Royal Shark (Book 6)

Rogue Prince (Book 7)

Rogue Gentleman (Book 8)

Rogue Rascal (Book 9)

Rogue Angel (Book 10)

Rogue Devil (Book 11)

Rogue Beast (Book 12)

Check out my website for the most up-to-date list of my books: kyliegilmore.com/books

ABOUT THE AUTHOR

Kylie Gilmore is the *USA Today* bestselling author of the Unleashed Romance series, the Rourkes series, the Happy Endings Book Club series, the Clover Park series, and the Clover Park STUDS series. She writes humorous romance that makes you laugh, cry, and reach for a cold glass of water.

Kylie lives in New York with her family, two cats, and a nutso dog. When she's not writing, reading hot romance, or dutifully taking notes at writing conferences, you can find her flexing her muscles all the way to the high cabinet for her secret chocolate stash.

Sign up for Kylie's Newsletter: https://www.kyliegilmore.com/FGnewsletter

For text alerts on Kylie's new releases, text KYLIE to the number 21000. (US only)

For more fun stuff check out Kylie's website https://www.kyliegilmore.com.

Thanks for reading *Fetching*. I hope you enjoyed it. Would you like to know about new releases? You can sign up for my new release email list at kyliegilmore.com/FGnewsletter. I promise not to clog your inbox! Only new release info, sales, and some fun giveaways.

I love to hear from readers! You can find me at:
kyliegilmore.com
Instagram.com/kyliegilmore
Facebook.com/KylieGilmoreToo
Twitter @KylieGilmoreToo

If you liked Wyatt and Sydney's story, please leave a review on your favorite retailer's website or Goodreads. Thank you.